Advanced Praise
The Ecology of Conversation

"Wow ... powerful ideas. Well written, fresh ... It made me want more. Quite intriguing."

Mary West Ferrell, M.S. Appalachian State University Professor

"Articulate, heartfelt, enthusiastic .... With a sense of energy and intimacy."

Barbara Mills, R.N., Ph.D. Clinical Psychologist

"I loved it! .... Has about twelve great insights per chapter."

Mary Willis, owner Montessori School

"OMG! I started learning about myself in the first chapter and continued right through to the end. Original material. Insightful. Powerful."

Diann Schindler, Ph.D. former community college president, President, Amelia Island Happenings

"What a pleasure! The Ecology of Conversation. *brings back many fond memories of the intensity, friendship and laughter with Judi and the other members of Executive Dinner Forum... Of particular impact is the concept of 'dialogue,' which has served me well since then. It's been invaluable in achieving insights and perspective, making me a better leader and person. If you're ready to realize the next level of leadership or personal development, this book can help you get there."*

George (Butch) Aggen, M.B.A. – former telecom executive, owner/ President, Goddard School

The Ecology of Conversation

~ Learning to Communicate From Your Core ~

Judith Beck, M.A.

Order this book online at www.trafford.com
or email orders@trafford.com

Most Trafford titles are also available at major online book retailers.

Printed in Victoria, BC, Canada.

ISBN: 978-1-4269-2331-9 (sc)
ISBN: 978-1-4269-2332-6 (hc)

Library of Congress Control Number: 2009913370

*Our mission is to efficiently provide the world's finest, most comprehensive book publishing
service, enabling every author to experience success. To find out how to publish your
book, your way, and have it available worldwide, visit us online at www.trafford.com*

Trafford rev. 2/9/10

North America & international
toll-free: 1 888 232 4444 (USA & Canada)
phone: 250 383 6864 ♦ fax: 812 355 4082

In Memory of my Dad
—Robert Cranston Utter—
on whose words I could always depend.

"As Above, So Below"

Table of Contents

Preface

My dog and I walk the same mountain trail every morning. At the trailhead, it is my custom to select a tall weed that has grown across or into my path. It must be at least three feet tall with a bushy top. I acknowledge its life—then break it off near its base. It becomes my cobweb catcher.

During this ritual, I ground myself for the day by immersing myself in nature: identifying bird calls, following animal tracks and even examining scat to try and detect who left it and what was digested! At the peak of the trail—my turn-around point—I discard the weed in the same pile and return down a cobweb-free trail. As the pile grows, I notice that some weeds immediately become brittle and brown, while others remain green and actually bloom a few days later. This oddity delights me.

In 23 years of working with people and groups, I notice that some whiz through the tough breaks—seemingly unaffected— and continue to thrive and bloom. Others become brittle and shrivel up. I've learned, however, that those who have become brittle can and do thrive again through some self-examination and a shift in perspective. They find their weed, clear their cobwebs and continue down the path of a life well-examined and well-lived.

This book is about clearing the cobwebs and thriving.

Enjoy.

Introduction

"In the seeing of who you are not, the reality of who you are emerges by itself."
Eckhart Tolle, A New Earth[1]

Authentic conversation—the kind where all participants are comfortable in their own skin and eager to exchange thoughts on what they know, feel or question—is a panacea. I crave this juicy genre of interaction—where we reveal our inner workings and share what's real, important, joyful, sad or confusing in our lives. I revel in the subsequent feelings of primal connectivity with the human race and feel cleansed when I've actively participated. From a personal satisfaction perspective, these conversations rank right up there with mutual intimacy with my partner, a great night's sleep, a wonderful book and adventure travel.

But great conversations create something even more enduring. They generate mutual learning, empathy, problem solving, conflict resolution, innovation and that ever-so-important sense of well-being and belonging that leads to a long and authentically lived life. For me, there is little more satisfying than an "a'ha" moment born of a group of openhearted, excited and committed people.

---

[1]   Tolle, Eckhart. A New Earth. NY: PLUME, 2006

Why do you suppose some of our most lively, salient, and heartfelt conversations are around a bottle of wine? Why are some of our best friendships generated in this scenario? Why do we require a relaxant to feel comfortable engaging with others on an intimate level? With the pleasure so palpable, why is this depth and freedom of expression so illusive?

We—in the Western world—have a multitude of answers, all of which carry seeds of truth:

- our culture of speed and competition—we're busy,
- families dotted all over the map—we're distant,
- frequent job switching—we're driven,
- a corporate climate of greed and stockholder value—we're guarded,
- a widening divide among political parties—we're angry,
- email, voicemail, text, Google—we're efficient and ... (dis)connected.

Yikes! Enough! Logical reasons all. But it doesn't make our deficiency of salient human interaction right. It just makes it dismally so.

When is the last time you sat down with others and said, let's really talk? Let's learn things from each other. Let's put our differences aside and create a new truth, new meaning? Let's evolve. I get excited just writing about it.

The Courage to Commit

The painful truth is—this is not easy to pull off. In fact, it seems to be getting more difficult. For this scenario to manifest, many things—that seem to be getting scarcer—are involved. To mention a few, transformational conversations require:

- time
- commitment
- real listening

- an open heart
- a beginner's mind
- awareness of one's preconceived notions
- a keen eye toward others' responses
- a desire to receive
- a desire to contribute
- the condition of equality

But most of all they require *courage*, the courage to reveal—and then loosen—one's hold on long held judgments and beliefs. This—most likely reluctant—*letting go* causes a blurring of one's identity. This blurring causes a battle with one's ego. This battle causes a barely conscious fear of losing oneself in the void—or looking just plain stupid. And this fear, Dear One, is the adversary of authentic interaction. We're afraid and possibly not even aware of our fear.

Yet many of us would rather live in a nebulous state of fear than open up to the gratification of an emotional, intellectual or spiritual world beyond our own. Good, bad, or indifferent—most of us are comfortable where we are. The challenge of rewarding conversation becomes: how does one overcome the fear of loss associated with acquiring the courage and *skill sets* necessary for deep and generative interactions? It begins here and now.

Why "The Ecology of Conversation?"

The Greek roots of the word ecology are ecos or oikos—translated as "home or place to live in;" and logos—translated as "word, thought, principle, study, speech." The word "ecology" is defined as the complex of relations between a specific organism and its environment. For our purposes, we are the organism—composed of mind and body—and our environment is the web of people around us—our relationships. So ecology—*in the pages that follow*—may be loosely translated as the study of the thoughts, principles and words that reside in us and thus influence our interactions with others.

The Latin roots of the word conversation are many—actually too many to cover in their entirety. But basically, the Latin for "con" means "with" or "jointly." And "vers" or "vert" mean "to turn." As such "conversare" is translated as "to turn to one another."

So the meaning of "The Ecology of Conversation" is to turn to oneself and others—that we might discover those influences, past and present, which are affecting our interactions with self and others.

Our ability to interact authentically—or not—is a reflection of these influences. Because we are conditioned to our own particular mindset, it takes commitment to gain awareness of the inner ecology of one's reactions and responses—especially those that are unconscious or automatic. It takes courage to question and eventually alter them. One may ask:

> How is my ego-mind translating a certain person, her actions or words?
>
> How will this message affect my responses to this person?
>
> How will it affect my ability to hear this person?
>
> How will it affect my ability to speak authentically to this person?
>
> From where did this conditioned response materialize?
>
> Can I accept that I may be wrong or that I have more to learn?
>
> What prejudices am I projecting onto this person or situation?

As you can see, deep and generative interaction is not simply a matter of honing one's listening or social skills. Rather, it requires knowing oneself well enough *to freely put that knowing aside.*

Inner Ecology – Outer Ecology

The pages that follow are in two sections and will move from microcosm (conversations with yourself) to macrocosm (conversations with others). In Part I, I encourage you to examine your inner ecology; e.g., "what ingrained messages involuntarily influence my interactions with others?" Its purpose is to shed light on your embedded and automatic responses. You'll gain conscious awareness of baggage, cultural influences and prejudices from your past, that are preventing you from moving forward in your quest for meaningful conversation and relationships today. This will be in the form of stories, information and self-exploratory activities. These are chapters 1–8.

In Part II, we move from inner ecology to outer ecology. Its purpose is to direct your newfound self-awareness toward deeper and more authentic interactions with others. In it, you will examine the energy of your thoughts on the spoken word. You will acquire generative conversational skills. You will gain the ability to let others into your hearts, where previously there was no room. You will improve your listening skills. I offer practical guidelines for practice and eventual mastery of deep and meaningful conversation. Finally, I suggest ways in which you might form your own group of committed conversationalists. These are chapters 9–16.

At the end of each chapter, I offer thought-questions relative to the subject matter. You are strongly encouraged to consider these questions and record your conclusions. Doing so will strengthen and solidify your learning experience. Some require little time—others require a great deal more, perhaps hours, days or weeks. Use your best judgment as to how much time you will invest. I believe that optimal learning will occur if you explore your answers and share your insights in a group setting. So consider forming a book club around <u>The Ecology of Conversation</u>. I suggest you buy a journal to record your thoughts, revelations and musings.

Proceed with Faith

I invite you to approach this book as an adventure into the unknown. Set aside preconceived notions and judgments about who you really are and what conversation really means. I suggest that you think of yourself as an explorer on a fascinating journey—where you have much to learn and everything to gain. You may encounter fog, detours, or stormy seas. I can't tell you precisely what you—or any one individual—will or will not discover. Simply be assured that any time one commits to a process with positive intent, good things follow. This has proven itself to me time and again.

I have embarked on many journeys of learning and self-discovery—sometimes on my own, sometimes as the requirement of a job. I have found that opening my heart to the process and approaching the curriculum without prejudice has opened doors unimagined. For instance, when my husband quit his salaried job to pursue art full time, I entered a state of insecurity and agitation. In my heart, I wanted him to follow his dreams. But in my head, I wanted to keep that second paycheck.

To prevent myself from sabotaging his efforts, I took a 12-week course on "The Artist's Way"—an exploration into creativity. My goal was to understand his motivations so I could relax and gain acceptance of our transition from a two-paycheck family to one—mine. I participated fully in the readings, activities and discussion—and fully enjoyed them. But in the spirit of authenticity, I must admit that at the end of the twelve weeks, I *still* had unfounded fears about our finances – and I was still pretty testy about his career move. That's the bad news.

The good news is ... I'd gained in three totally unanticipated ways. One—I got my first magazine article published in an international publication. Two—I applied for and was invited to lead a workshop at a national conference of human resource professionals. Three—I began the process of forgiving and healing a challenging relationship with a family member. Whew!

Though wholly unplanned and unexpected, these outcomes were far more life-altering than my short-term goal of easing my anxiety over money. In retrospect, I realize that it was *change* I feared, not decreased income. Erase those twelve weeks and I might not be writing this book. I might still be at odds with my family member. I certainly wouldn't have made the leaps and bounds in my career as human resource consultant. As the country Western song goes; "some of God's greatest gifts are unanswered prayers.[2]" This sentiment has been a constant in my life.

So, I humbly challenge and implore you, if you want to know yourself better and if you, like I, crave engagement in more meaningful conversations and intimate relationships, commit to this journey—and beyond. Complete the exercises. Maintain an open mind. Chart you discoveries along the way. Try new things—always with love for yourself and others. But, above all have faith in the outcome—in whatever form it takes.

Bon Voyage Dear One!

"Life shrinks or expands in proportion to one's courage."
Anais Nin, The Diary of Anais Nin, Vol. 3[3]

[2]   Brooks, Garth "Unanswered Prayers," *No Fences*. Capitol Records, Nashville, 1998.

[3]   Nin, Anais. The Diary of Anais Nin, Vol. 3. Boston, MA: Harcourt, 1971.

A Word With Book Groups

Hi! I'm so pleased that you have decided to join together around The Ecology of Conversation. Though certainly not essential, I believe reading and processing the book—as a group—will result in more enlightenment, growth and enjoyment.

You have many options before you. You can convene a group of strangers by advertising in a publication or bulletin board. Or you can gather a group of friends, colleagues, family—or friends and their friends, family and colleagues! Whichever format piques your fancy, I encourage you to follow through. Your group can be as small as three members or as many as 18 or 20.

Diversity of membership is great—really great. The more diverse your group, the more insights await you. So go nuts. Welcome people of different ages, colors, sexes, cultures, sexual preferences and religions. The more ingredients in the mix, the more savory your stew will be.

I suggest you meet weekly or biweekly. Everyone read a chapter and complete the exercises prior to each meeting. Then share your insights during your gathering. You can follow the format in chapter 14 or devise your own protocol. But essentially if you: check-in[4], share answers to questions at the end of the chapters, acknowledge commonalities, share insights, and adjourn—you'll be on the right path. Depending on the size of

---

[4]   Check-in essentially answers the question "how are you?"

your group, one and one-half to two hours of conversation—per chapter—should suffice.

Take turns facilitating. Because a facilitator should remain objective, (s)he has a different experience from the other participants. Choose to facilitate when you're not overly invested in the contents of a chapter. This way you won't be burning to contribute when your role is to make sure everyone *else* is contributing. *A facilitator's role is to ask questions—not answer them.* E.g., you don't need to know the answers—you just need to ask the questions so the group can discover the answers. If your members don't want to facilitate, recruit someone to do so. Make sure that person's motive is completely free of personal agenda.

Use the first meeting to get to know one another and devise your own guidelines for conversation. For example, your guidelines might include: share airtime, listen intently, speak from your heart, reserve judgment, find commonalities, seek to understand, be alert to new insights, etc!

Your first meeting or two may be awkward. This is natural. Reserve judgment and carry on. I find delightful surprises in every endeavor of this kind. And often I become good friends with the very person who annoyed me in the first meeting. So have faith.

And have fun.

Part One

Inner Ecology

"On the Trail"

Chapter 1

The Ecology of Fear

"The heaviest thing in your backpack is fear."
Marcia

I have a friend who completed the last leg of the Appalachian Trail in 2008. She walked it alone. It took years because she did it in segments between jobs and vacations. If anyone is an expert on packing for the trail, it is she.

The Backpack

We were talking just before she was preparing for the final leg. She related how each time became easier. She stopped anticipating encounters with bears or strangers. She now slept restfully by herself in the wilderness. She welcomed the solitude and countless steps of interchangeable terrain and scenery. She anticipated the fatigue and boredom of the hike. She knew the best antidotes for blisters, bugs, bumps and bruises. She had quit packing for every possible emergency—content that she was resourceful enough and the world was abundant enough that she could make do in the unlikely event that some calamity should befall her. Year after year, her load became lighter and lighter

1

until, finally, she was able to complete the trail unencumbered by any excess weight, whatsoever.

"The heaviest thing in your backpack is fear," she eventually concluded.

This statement stopped me dead in my tracks. On a very practical level, I recalled all the trips I'd taken where I simply had to add one more thing to my luggage. Then one more, then one more—just incase. Yet, I traveled in a five-seater plane to the Corcovado Rain Forest in Costa Rica. Each passenger was allowed only 20 pounds of luggage. I packed lean and mean. During the subsequent ten-day sojourn, I lacked for nothing. So, materialistically, I related completely to her observation.

But the statement carries a one-two punch. And it is the metaphorical basis for the pages that follow. Life is a journey with ups and downs—mountains, valleys, rocks, roots, weather, rodents and water-crossings. Just like the Appalachian Trail, there is potential for peril or pleasure at every turn. The heavier one's backpack, the greater potential for harm. At a physical level, added pounds add more pressure to your joints and muscles, creating an environment for repetitive motion injury. Plus, you're more likely to trip on a root or slip on a rock if you're more fatigued from carrying extra weight. Physical fatigue contributes to mental fatigue, so you're more likely to make the wrong decision when encountering a tenuous situation.

And what about fun along the way? How much can you have when you're so encumbered by the weight of all that baggage?

So it is with the weight of our fears. Metaphorically speaking, I would hazard to guess it is the heaviest burden that you or I carry.

When my husband, Kevin began his career in fulltime art, I had fears of a change in lifestyle and diminishing savings. I feared I would resent him because I'd be carrying the burden of income while he got his feet on the ground. I feared our marriage might not survive the transition. I feared getting in the way of his happiness. Most of all, I feared I was being unreasonable!

The more fear I acquired, the tenser I became. As Charlie Brown (from the Peanuts comic strip) would exclaim when he's reached the boiling point, "Agh!!!!" I needed perspective. I needed to embrace the truth of our situation, which didn't merit the weight of my fears.

What's the Worst That Can Happen?

Everyone has his or her own brand of fearfulness: violent weather, strangers, public speaking, reptiles, crowds. I can't relate to these because I have my own set of fears! When I was in sales, for instance, I dreaded picking up the phone and making a cold call. I would find every task that needed done—and then invent more—just to avoid the act. I would secretly hope that my prospect wouldn't be there so I could just leave a message. Maybe then they would call *me* back. But then I wouldn't be prepared—I'd be caught off guard. Oh, no! Better just to bite the bullet and try my best to get through.

There were several techniques I'd use to prepare for these calls. Sometimes I'd envision a mountain; I wanted to reach the top—for the view—but I couldn't get there until I did the hard work of climbing. "Climbing" equaled making the call. While dialing, I'd envision myself atop a gorgeous vista, breathing the fresh air and enjoying the view. Other times I'd ask myself; "OK Judi, what is the worst thing that could happen if you make this call?" Of course, the worst thing was someone saying they're not interested or—God forbid—hanging up on me. Well, how bad is that? That wouldn't kill me, I'd tell myself.

The vast majority of people on the other end of the phone line were courteous, if not delightful. The more delightful people I spoke with, the more delightful I became. The more delightful I became, the better the outcome of the calls. I became almost weightless with delight. Yet, I began my day sweating and stewing over the 1 or 2 percent who might be unpleasant with me. What a waste!

Fear is a heavy burden that prevents us from experiencing so much beauty, connection and joy.

Stop reading at the end of this paragraph. Take several deep breaths. Stretch. Get a drink of water. Take a walk around your yard or living space. Retrieve pen and pad or journal. In it, take stock of the contents of your "backpack." Make a list of at least ten fears that cloud your thinking, perceiving and reacting. They may revolve around money, health, relationships, religion, work or natural disaster! For example: you may be afraid of: going back to school, asking for a raise, meeting minorities, going to Hell, windstorms, etc. You'll know them when you *feel* them. Mine become apparent with tightness just above my sternum and a bit toward my heart. Yours' may present themselves as a throbbing in your temple or a knot in your stomach. Trust these messages. Be brutally honest. Record them faithfully. If you feel hesitancy, all the more reason to take note. If you're stumped, walk away and reconsider later. Scary? Yes? Be courageous!

When you've completed your list, take a few deep, deliberate breaths. Inhale the present moment to the count of 15. Then exhale the past to the count of 10. Repeat at least twice. Welcome back.

Chapter 2

The Ecology of Authenticity

"It's not the things I've gone and done I regret or feel ashamed. It's the things I didn't say or do just because I was afraid. Just because I was afraid."
"The Things I've Gone and Done," Carrie Newcomer[5]

We might as well face it. Truth telling takes courage—a heck of a lot sometimes. A new book by Robert Feldman (<u>The Liar in Your Life</u>)[6] concludes that in the first ten minutes of meeting someone new, we tell—on average—three lies. It's a cultural norm. So don't even try to exclude yourself from this statistic. We want to be cordial so we tell someone it's nice meeting him or her—even if it isn't. If we don't want to accept an invitation, we say we have a doctor's appointment or simply "forget" to respond at all. We want to be independent so we say "no" when what we really feel is "yes, yes, I need your help!" Or we say "yes" when it would feed our spirit to say "no thanks, that just doesn't feel right for me." It's an epidemic.

---

5   Newcomer, Carrie. (and Mark Williams), "The Things I've Gone and Done, "*The Gathering of Spirits*.2002, BMI, Bloomington, IN.

6   Feldman, Robert. <u>The Liar in Your Life</u>. NY: Virgin Books, 2009.

When I find myself falling into this pretense, I actually feel the physical weight of having to remember what I said. Or I feel the sadness of not respecting myself or the other enough to be honest. I feel the shame of my lack of courage. I feel the loss of an authentic life. What have I to fear by simply telling the truth?

Ray

One of the most exhilarating relationships I've experienced was with a colleague named Ray. I actually thought he was nuts when we first met. He had this untamed demeanor. He had a perpetual smile. His eyes were bright and a little wild. He said outrageous things. He talked about poop in public, for God's sake! He was entering my field—corporate development and teambuilding—and he wanted to collaborate with me. Truth be told, I thought he was a loose cannon and I avoided him. I certainly didn't want to expose *my* clients to him. So instead of getting mad, he contracted me to work with him and his new clients. We began a collaborative consulting relationship.

Freelancing in corporate development frequently means traveling with colleagues to distant locales and spending lots of time together. You can't help but get to know one another well. Spending time with Ray was always a novelty. It was always educational. It was always poignant and often exhilarating.

As you've probably surmised, he was an unabashed truth teller. He could tell a team of executives that they were full of s--t and everybody would laugh and fall off their chairs. He was positively exuberant in his truth telling—his backpack was so light that he barely touched the ground. And it was contagious. The more truth he told, the more I told, the more our clients told. Oh, my God—they were truth fests! What's more, we were able to show vulnerability and laugh at our silly selves—anytime. Like the lady in the movie, "When Harry Met Sally," I decided I wanted what he had.

The catch was…Ray had an untreatable brain tumor. He kept a removable plate in his head so surgeons could remove parts of the tumor when it got too big. It would grow in different directions each time and stimulate different parts of his brain. One time he discovered that he could fall into trance and *speak in tongues*. What's more, when he became agitated—or couldn't sleep—he found that doing so relieved his anxiety. He offered to show me how it manifested. I must say that the prospect of "losing" Ray—if only for a few minutes—felt more than a little precarious. Yet, I didn't want to pass up this opportunity. I vacillated. Finally I said "yes."

He took a few quiet moments to gather himself. Then suddenly this strong, attractive, vibrant man became something alien and otherworldly as the incomprehensible "words" spilled from him. I watched in awe as he demonstrated, in very graphic fashion, a symptom of the aggressor that was growing within him—and spilling forth in this eerie incantation. After a few minutes, he returned to the Ray I knew—if perhaps a little weary. His smile was a little less toothy, his eyes a bit glazed. But as always, I celebrated his ability to embrace his fears and reveal his truth with such integrity, passion and trust. Our friendship grew, together with my admiration for his strength of character.

Authentic Presence

He called his programs "authentic presence." Corporations enrolled executives so they might become more aware of themselves and others. They were wildly successful. From Ray, I—and others—learned not to wait until we're dying to experience "the lightness of being"[7] that resulted from facing our fears and being ourselves. We learned that vulnerability was a positive trait and that truth telling was a bridge to connection with others. I learned that—as much as our culture dictates that we be strong and self-reliant, we are stronger and more fulfilled within the

---

[7] Borrowed from the book (and movie of the same name) "The Incredible Lightness of Being" by Milan Kunndera (Harper & Rowe, NY, 1984).

realm of "tribe." We're not independent—we're *inter*dependent. From his diseased ecology, he granted others nourishment, connection and well-being.

But authenticity is still an arduous journey. Going against the cultural norms of conformity, self-reliance and white lies can be daunting and sticky. And sometimes, in spite of my best intentions, I regress. Ray died from his tumor in 1999. He worked with clients until a week before his death. I miss his honesty, his courage, his generosity of spirit, his interdependence and his joie de vivre. He was a role model for anyone seeking deeper and wider roots.

Stop reading at the end of this paragraph. Get a drink of water. Stretch. Take a few deep breaths. Walk around your yard or living space. Retrieve a pen and your pad or journal. Go back to your list from chapter 1 and re-imagine how you would feel if you had a way of embracing, celebrating and communicating your hopes, desires and fears in loving, boisterous and thoughtful ways—the way Ray did. Answer questions like: what do I choose to hide, why do I hide it, how might others and I benefit if I reveal my inner truths? On what occasions do I say yes when I really mean no—or vice versa?

Be brutally honest with yourself and take the time necessary for this exercise. Walk away and come back tomorrow, if necessary. This is the first step to "authentic presence." After all, if you can't be honest with yourself, you certainly can't experience the exhilaration of being honest with others. Imagine the feeling in your gut after you've exposed a truth and had it well received— by you or others. Write down how you feel after simply telling your truths.

Chapter 3

The Ecology of Perception

"We don't see things as they are, we see things as we are."
Anais Nin, The Diary of Anais Nin, Vol. 3[8]

We're all different.

It isn't enough that we have completely different DNA. We also grew up in different circumstances, with different parents, birth order, teachers, friends, clergy, etc! It's no surprise then, that we receive, interpret and regurgitate information differently.

The Road Trip

I was on a road trip with a married couple for seven hours once. They sat in the front seat. I sat in the back. He inquired about my field of study, which was ecopsychology. The inquiry turned into an invigorating seven-hour dialogue where he challenged every tenet of my thesis and I responded fervently. It was positively exhilarating having someone so engaged in

---

[8] Nin, Anais. The Diary of Anais Nin, Vol. 3. Boston, MA: Harcourt, 1971.

something I was passionate about. The seven-hour trip flew by and he and I established a bond that was not present before.

Over a year later, the three of us reconvened at a party. In the course of our conversation, "Bill" and I referred back to our conversation in the car that day. "Jenny" immediately bristled—her eyes blazing—and yelled, "Stop! I can't stand to hear you two argue anymore—that was the most stressful seven hours of my life!"

I stared at her aghast. Because she was in the front seat and couldn't always see my expression, she thought her husband had maligned me for the whole trip. She misinterpreted my passionate responses as anger. She couldn't believe that I was even speaking to her husband after "what he'd done." I also believe she wasn't acculturated to the brand of back and forth that her husband and I shared that day. She'd probably seen him offend others with similar behavior. Not me. I was enlivened.

She had projected *her* feelings onto *me*.

I Could Never Say That

Another story stands out in my mind. I facilitated an "Executive Dinner Forum" for many years in the 1990's. Its members were high-level executives from different companies and industries. The function of the group was to discuss, dissect and evolve issues that were indigenous to the leadership role. Each month a different member chose the topic. That particular month, the topic was "security." A CEO who was considering retirement and wanted feedback on the mental, emotional and financial aspects of his transition chose it.

We always began with a leading question. That evening, we asked of one another, "what does security mean to you?" Each member responded similarly with the common theme of financial stability for themselves and their families. As facilitator, I only contributed to the discussion if I felt the group was stuck or too homogeneous in their thinking. This appeared to be the case.

So, to stimulate them a bit more, I offered my definition. "My security comes with knowing I have a healthy mind and body—and also knowing that when I walk out my door each morning, there is no war, pestilence or violence awaiting me."

Immediately "Sarah," the only other woman in the group—and with whom I was generally "in sync"—began shaking her head vigorously.

"I could never say that, Judi. I'll never have that sense of security!" Mind you, this woman lived in a fabulous neighborhood, inside the beltline. Her husband was similarly successful in his job. Her two kids attended private school. She had a full-time housekeeper and drove an expensive sports car. All mouths dropped and we stared in amazement as she continued.

"No Jew with any sense of history can feel that sense of security. Rational or not, I fear opening my door in the morning. I fear for my children at school. It's almost innate in my culture."

I saw things as I was. She saw things as she was. Until that moment, I had minimal appreciation of the deep cultural and perceptual divide between us. But through the giving and receiving of information, I understood more of her story and thus, became a little worldlier.

It is said, "perception is reality." In each of the previous stories, *my* perception was *my* reality—until I heard the reality of others. Then I realized there were, indeed, dual realities in our differing perspectives. These are not isolated incidents. Multiple realities are all around us—all the time. Different people live different realities. Our ability to share diverse views and experiences allows us to recognize and appreciate these dualities, thereby allowing our relationships to grow, evolve and thrive.

Our human ecosystem thrives on diversity. Like a virgin forest or pristine waterway that hasn't been altered by the actions of man, we humans grow in health and well-being when learning from those with perspectives different from our own.

Stop reading at the end of this paragraph. Get a drink of water. Stretch. Take a few deep breaths. Walk around your yard or living space. Retrieve your pen and pad or journal. Make a list of conversations or events from your past that were left hanging and you now believe are open for re-interpretation. These may take a couple of hours or days for you to recall. That's OK. Ask yourself questions like: what else could this mean, did I respond appropriately, how did my particular viewpoint color my interpretation? Place a star next to those that you now believe might tell a different tale. Aren't you curious?

Knowing with certainty that your interpretation is *always* different—in ways great or small—gives you immediate breathing room and opens the door for more authentic and evolved interaction. Simply stay with these scenarios without interpretation or judgment. Open your mind to other possibilities. It should feel bright and expansive.

Chapter 4

The Ecology of Judgment

"Love always challenges you to be flexible about your beliefs and let others into your heart."
Paul Ferrini, Silence of the Heart[9]

Since we were children, most of us have believed that we were the center of the universe.

Granted, we're mostly unaware of this belief. But think about it. In your heart of hearts, don't you sometimes believe that you have more influence, knowledge, experience or common sense than anyone else in a room full of people? Don't you believe that: your political beliefs are wisest, your child-rearing techniques are best, and your directions to the airport are fastest? Congratulations—you have a healthy self-esteem. But, your dogged self-assuredness is also *blocking flows of information into your life*. And when one does this, s/he blocks all the wonderful side effects of that information, as well.

[9]   Ferrini, Paul. Silence of the Heart. Greenfield, MA: Heartways Press, 1996.

Will I Go Flat?

I'm reminded of the story of the toddler charging to his mother, finger extended and tears spurting from his eyes. On his finger is a droplet of blood—the result of an encounter with a thorn bush. "Honey! It's OK. It's only a drop of blood. Let me get a band aid." The child's wailing escalates. "Calm down! It's only a pinprick." Sputter, spurt, cough, hiccup. "It's nothing. Be a brave boy!" Wahhh!!! Finally, in a moment of irritation, "Honey what is it?!"

"Mom, will I go flat?"

By projecting her adult reactions to a droplet of blood, Mom blocked access to her son's real concern—going flat.

Now, it's probably relatively easy to put yourself in the place of the mother, chastise yourself for your jump to judgment, and alter your opinion of this encounter. In the child's innocence, he feared losing volume in his finger! How could you know that? He's just an innocent, after all. Your ego remains intact.

But, what if the misunderstanding is with someone other than a child—a total stranger who is tailgating you while you're going the speed limit? Or a distracted bank teller who's taking more time than necessary to complete a transaction? Or even someone who picked your pocket in the grocery store? What are their stories?

Is the tailgater trying desperately to catch up with her husband who left important documents on the kitchen counter? Is the bank teller recovering from an encounter with a short-change artist? Is the thief desperately trying to provide for his family at Christmas after losing his job in November? I call this type of reassessment "re-imagining."

Beyond the momentary irritation of these scenarios, what about a colleague you observe doing freelance work at his regular job, a spouse with incompatible child-rearing standards, a neighbor whose yard is in a perpetual state of disarray? These can affect your sense of identity and standards of right and wrong.

Re-imagining these scenarios doesn't necessarily make any of them right. Each, at first glance anyhow, is annoying at best. But what's right about re-imagining is *how it makes you feel.* By giving others the benefit of the doubt, you can often continue with your life, having felt empathy, rather than wrath.

To allow himself this time, the freelancer may have stayed late last night. The spouse is a product of the child-rearing s/he received and is doing the best s/he can. The messy neighbor may have a parent in crisis and spends every weekend with her— instead of caring for his yard.

As much as our ego tries to convince us otherwise, *we simply don't know* the cause and effect of others' behaviors. And it does us no good to judge.

This isn't a medical book—but one could argue that one's health and well-being depends on developing the skill of lassoing our "judgment gene" and instead, re-imagining a more benevolent scenario. For, the unresolved anger, accelerated pulse and rise in blood pressure—that often accompany a rush to condemnation cause release of the stress hormone cortisol—which is associated with a higher probability of heart disease. And, according to research done through the Institute of HeartMath, an oversupply of cortisol is also injurious to the brain, the hormonal and immune systems.

Conversely, experiencing feelings of care and compassion can actually reverse these effects by increasing the flow of DHEA and IgA into the system. DHEA is often referred to as the anti-aging hormone and IgA (immunoglobulin A) is known to boost one's immune system (Doc Childre, <u>Freeze Frame</u>, pgs. 39–42).[10]

You may rightly conclude the practice of compassionate thinking is good for your health.

---

[10] Childre, Doc. <u>Freeze Frame</u>. Boulder, MA: Planetary Publications, 1994, 1998.

Re-Imagining

I was hired to work with a young woman who is a valuable employee of one of my corporate clients. She is ardently religious and had very specific—some might say rigid—beliefs about the nature of man as inherently evil. Under stress, these beliefs were intensified and she became rude and haughty to colleagues and customers—envisioning those who irritated her to be embodying their original sin. Several had been hurt, angered or offended by her behavior—and had subsequently complained to management. When she began her sentences with "oh, my sweet Delilah ..." everyone ran for cover. Unable to control her stress or challenge the tenets of her church, she was teetering on the precipice of losing her job. She'd come to the end of her rope.

We worked intensely together in two sessions. Among other things, it became clear that as long as she felt that *everyone* (including herself) was inherently evil, each time she became stressed, she would revert to this disagreeable behavior. I decided to attempt to help her to re-imagine the concept of "evil."

Together, we brainstormed the possibilities. She struggled to loosen her grip on these long held beliefs. But eventually, we came up with replacement sentiments for the word, such as: "weak, troubled, sad, misguided, searching, and immature."

Sometime during this re-imagining exercise, her features *visibly* softened; the welts that had formed on her neck disappeared; her body relaxed and her eyes cleared. Her wrath was being replaced with empathy. By amending her definition of "evil," she recovered physically, as well as emotionally, from her torment. From a very deep level, I saw that she was not only reforming judgments about her colleagues and customers, *she was forgiving herself*. Her "ecosystem" became self-sustaining once again. She has been a happier and more forgiving person since then. She looks years younger and remains at her job.

Stop reading at the end of this paragraph. Get a drink of water. Stretch. Take a few deep breaths. Walk around your yard or living space. Retrieve your pen and pad or journal. Make a list of 5 long held personal beliefs that you feel are due for reassessment. They may include self-judgments that inhibit your freedom of expression—or other-judgments that prevent you from relating well with certain segments of the population. For example: women can't be trusted; I'll never find happiness; dogs will always bite. Now re-imagine the meaning of each sentiment. Ask questions like: might I reassess this conclusion? Does this belief serve me? Would my higher self or a higher power support this thinking?

Recalling these may take minutes, hours or days. Stay with it. Share your insights. Don't be afraid—these aren't written in blood. Go for it! This is about loosening your hold of rigid views on life, love and the human condition. You'll feel better about yourself—physically, emotionally and spiritually—when you're finished.

Chapter 5

The Ecology of Letting Go

"Only when you think and act beyond your immediate ego needs does your
life become subject to the law of grace."
Paul Ferrini, Silence of the Heart [11]

How are you feeling having completed the previous exercise?
Do you feel lighter or freer? If so, congratulations are in order.
It means you're puncturing that part of your ego that holds and
protects you from "being wrong" or "being less than." Ouch!
We all truly hate those feelings. But, realizing there are alternative
"truths" frees you from rigid thinking and provides more
opportunity for heartfelt connection with others. Carry on.

The Apology

A short time ago I had a small CD mature. I looked up my
paperwork so I'd know how much interest to expect. I left the
paperwork at home and proceeded to the bank with a figure in
mind. When the teller calculated it, it was considerably less than
my accounting. I talked to the bank manager who said she'd
research it and figure it out for me. In the meantime, I went

---

[11]   Ferrini, Paul. Silence of the Heart. Greenfield, MA: Heartways
Press, 1996.

to the grocery store, content that when I returned I'd receive a check in the right amount.

When I returned, I saw the manager through the glass wall of her office. She avoided my gaze. Nuts. Clearly she was agitated that she had to address a difference of opinion. Already in defensive armor, she produced the interest rate figures for the date I had purchased the CD. It didn't match up with my "data." Not even close. The tension rose and neither of us was very pleasant. She tersely insisted I produce the agreement that I had left at home. I agreed to fax it to her—"so I wouldn't have to make another trip into town." Now I had two reasons to be mad—the money and her "rudeness."

You guessed it. When I retrieved the agreement and read the fine print, I realized that I was wrong. The paperwork I had was from the original three-month agreement I'd contracted six months ago. I had renewed "at current rates" for three more months and those were considerably less. When I looked over the agreement, I saw that I'd hand-scratched the new rate right there on the page! Oh, I was so wrong! Now I was *really* mad about her "lack of customer service." I faxed the page to her and requested she send me the check.

When she called to tell me what I already knew, I'd had time to swallow some of my pride. I stopped her and said, "I know. I was wrong and you were right. I'm sorry." I heard a relieved exhalation from her end of the phone. The amazing thing is—once these dreaded words popped out of my mouth, I realized that my fears of being wrong and appearing stupid were unfounded. My ego remained intact and it didn't hurt at all. In fact, it felt great! Who'd have thought admitting a wrong could feel so good? Yet, we still resist this admission like the plague.

There's an old saying that I adhere to: "Would you rather be right or happy?" I choose happy.

Getting Down to Business

A married couple, "John" and "Julie," own a business they've operated for 20 years. He runs the day-to-day operations; she does behind the scenes tasks. We became acquainted when my husband and I moved to the area. Before we got to know them well, their business experienced some turmoil due to changes in government regulations. John hired me to work with his staff in order to better address and adapt to the new criteria. As preparation, I asked to interview key stakeholders in the business: managers, longtime employees and key contributors. So, he made a list for me to draw from. I subsequently queried all the people on the list and then proposed an intervention.

Shortly thereafter, I got a tearful and despondent call from Julie. To my horror and utter embarrassment, I learned that not only was she the *president of the company*, she also founded and operated it for its' first several years! At the time she was doing accounts receivable and payable (from home), some of the hiring (offsite) and a portion of the buying. Since I'd never seen her at the business and hadn't been told of her role, I had no idea that she was, indeed, also a stakeholder. She had not been on my list.

Such a thorny predicament. I swallowed some rising panic and apologized profusely—trying not to implicate her husband and business partner. But, from my point of view, she had valid justification to fire me on the spot.

I braced myself for the worst. To her immense credit and my great relief, she accepted my apology and simply got down to business. She placed none of the blame on me—though I still believe I deserved some. Rather, she asked to be included in the interviews. We set up an appointment, I completed the inquiry with *all* stakeholders and the intervention proceeded, as planned. Since then, the business *and* our friendship have prospered.

More importantly, from a personal perspective, I experienced the grace of someone who understood that ego was less important than making things right. She could have fired me for overlooking her. She could have blamed her husband or their employees. She could have raised a huge fracas and no one would have blamed her, including me. But instead, she recognized what was needed at the moment—and acted on it. After the intervention, we both moved forward, not only with the business, but also with our friendship. Today she has a far greater presence in the day-to-day operations of their successful business.

Developing the ability to manage one's ego—as Julie did—is extraordinary. Surely she was wounded—as anyone would be. But she recognized the complexity of the situation and acknowledged her role in the mix-up. Rather than rant and rave about exclusion or injustice, she simply stated her case and initiated steps to righting a wrong. What self-possession. What a gift. What a role model she is.

Stop reading at the end of this paragraph. Get a drink of water. Take a few deep breaths. Stretch. Walk around your yard or living space. Retrieve your pen and pad or journal. Then consider; are there apologies left suspended in your life that you should be extending? Make a list of a few of them and write the best and worst things that could happen if you actually initiate them. Take your time. Now, I encourage you to act on *at least* one of these. If you're hesitant, start small—like when you snapped at someone or forgot to return a phone call. Please—be sure to apologize with your whole heart. This means *admitting you were wrong, acknowledging and accepting responsibility for hurt feelings and sincerely asking for forgiveness.* Please! Don't apologize like a politician—you *know* what I mean.

But just in case you don't know, here's how we've come to expect a politician to apologize for indiscretions. "*If* I did something wrong, I'm sorry." This is not an apology.

P.S. To the politicians out there who know how to apologize— and I know there are many of you; I'm very sorry for stereotyping you. I know you're not all alike. I've surely offended you. Please forgive me for my injudiciousness. And thank you for being a role model for sincere and heartfelt apologies.

Chapter 6

The Ecology of Story

Stories… "heal when they are more about who we are, not what we have done. About what we have faced to build what we have, what we have drawn upon and risked to do, what we have felt, thought, feared and discovered through the events of our lives."
Rachel Naomi Remen, <u>Kitchen Table Wisdom</u>[12]

One-Minute-Stories

We've been getting acquainted with the "shadow" side of our egos—those unexamined psychic messages that burden our interpersonal relations. Through my own and others' stories, we've been addressing our subjective interpretations of people's words and actions. We've been discovering what influences from our past color those interpretations.

But what about *your* stories? Which ones define you and which are most apt to influence your judgment of others?

The famous avant-garde composer, John Cage was scheduled to give a lecture at the Brussels Fair in 1958. In contemplating

---

[12]   Remen, Rachel Naomi. <u>Kitchen Table Wisdom</u>. NY: Riverhead Books, 1996.

the content of his speech, he recalled a suggestion from a friend years earlier—that he should give a talk with nothing but stories as its content. He decided to do so.

A little background on this colorful man. As an avant-garde artist, John composed "music" with no harmony and no apparent beat or synchrony. Rather, his musical score often included sounds from the environment (radio static, pots and pans, burps) or notes *chosen merely by chance*—with the suggestion that everything is related whether we know it or not. As such, he decided to write stories of his life and from his memory—*at random*—and then deliver them, one after the other, in one-minute segments at the Brussels Fair. On this occasion, the Brussels audience heard 30 of John's stories in 30 minutes. Then he walked off the stage.

Upon reading this account in his book, Silence,[13] I dubbed them one-minute-stories. This concept was so attractive to me that I began writing my own one-minute-stories, at will. This was in 1993. Mind you, many are simply snippets of the life and times of a girl/woman growing up in the Midwest: family, college, marriage, moving south, professional life, etc. But, others stand out. These are poignant and all encompassing—and influenced me in profound ways. I call these the "stories of my life." Recalled at random, in the course of writing—these gems emerged as the clay that sculpted the woman that I've become.

A Child's Eyes—A Woman's Eyes

For instance, I recall a family road trip—in the 60's—from the south of Michigan (where we lived) to the northern shores of Lake Michigan, where we had a cabin. What is now a five-hour drive was then upwards of 12 hours. As such, the family—led by my Dad—would make frequent stops in small towns—to rest and refresh. Coffee and doughnuts from family-owned diners were the menu items of choice. Despite the goodies, I disliked

---

[13] Cage, John. Silence. Middletown, CT: Wesleyan University Press, 1961.

the stops because I just wanted to get there! My dad, on the other hand, loved the exploratory aspect of this ritual. On one such stop, I remember getting impatient because he was engaged with a street-sweeper. The two men were lost in conversation, sweeping gestures, smiles and laughter. Why, I thought, is he even paying attention to someone of such lowly status, let alone holding us up and adding minutes to our drive?

As I watched impatiently, I must've noticed the sparkle in my Dad's eyes, his relaxed stance leading up to vacation after months of hard work, and his joy in making a new "friend"—because that's what I recall today. In recalling the instant, the feelings of a frustrated adolescent have been replaced by the affections of a woman. For, I'm aware that this was one of Dad's many legacies to me—a joie de vivre, the ability to find commonality with others and an open heart. Because I've acquired these character traits, I've identified this brief "story" as a life-defining moment. I'm unabashedly grateful for its retrieval and the self-awareness it has afforded me.

Story is one of our most powerful tools in gaining *self and other*-awareness. The challenge is to continue growing and developing without necessarily *becoming* our stories—in particular, the negative ones. For, if allowed, these can impede us for life. Rather, by recalling them, one has the opportunity to learn and then set them aside—or embrace and cherish them like a favorite pillow. We want our stories to be bridges, not barriers.

What stories from your past, do you tell and retell? Are they affirmations or defamations? Do you wallow in them or revel in them? Do they connect or obstruct?

Eloquence or Connectivity?

If you heard Barack Obama's keynote address at the 2004 Democratic National Convention or his speech on race, leading up to the 2008 election, you've heard many of the defining *one-minute-stories* of his life. Love or hate the Democratic platform, many were still moved by his stories of bi-racial parentage, identity struggles, early loss of both parents, rearing by grandparents, and moves from Hawaii to Malaysia to Kansas—all in the course of a childhood. Not to mention the stories of his courtship, marriage and bearing of his own children. They were heartfelt, philosophical and genuine. I would venture to say that it wasn't so much his much-touted "eloquence" that clinched his election. Rather, it was the familiarity and intimacy generated by the telling of his stories. We related and connected to the human being.

I find the experience of telling my stories—and hearing others'—therapeutic and continue to record them today. If I can become aware of stories' influence on me, I can tread the path of lifelong growing and learning. I can decide to capitalize on their lessons—or commit to assuaging a negative past. We want our stories to be bridges, not barriers. Stories point the way for ongoing growth and development. They also open doors for intimacy with others. Clearly this awareness is *everything*.

Diamonds in the Sunlight

I never got to see or hear John Cage in person. But, I'm fortunate that I got to attend a performance by his creative and life-partner, Merce Cunningham. Merce was a dancer and choreographer. True to the avant-garde movement, his dance company performed to music *unrelated to the dance*. In other words, his dancers *practiced* their performance without any accompaniment, whatsoever. On the night of the show, they performed to whatever "music" was provided! Often times it was the first time they'd seen the set, as well. Just imagine the dancers, dancing to disparate music and occasionally crashing into the props or each other—because the stage was bare when they practiced.

At first, the viewer is struck by the utter chaos of it all. Music, dance, props—nothing makes sense. But the longer you watch, the more often you discover moments—just moments—of pure brilliance, clarity and synchrony. At these moments, everything coalesces with dancer, music and set achieving divine perfection. It is delightful. It's magic.

This is what happens while writing one-minute-stories. Most, while memorable, have little meaning. But every once in a while, one stands out like a diamond in the sunlight. You know immediately that *this* is a story of your life. Over time and space, you stitch together a patchwork quilt—of little gems— that reveals your whole story. It's a masterpiece. And you are the star.

Stop reading at the end of this paragraph. Get a drink of water. Take a few deep breaths. Stretch. Walk around your yard or living space. Now sit down with pen and pad or journal. Begin recalling the stories of your life. Do this in no particular order or fashion. You can continue this for days or years! But begin now. Resist judging or compartmentalizing them. When you think of a story, write it down and don't quit 'til you are finished. Remember—these are one-minute-stories. Keep them brief. And have fun. Your tapestry will be beautiful.

Chapter 7

The Ecology of Now

Where are you? What time is it? Who are you?
"The Peaceful Warrior," 2006

Have you ever noticed how everyone interprets the same moment differently? Ask any three witnesses to an event—even your own stories—and each will be recalled differently.

My husband and I watched a thought-provoking movie recently. The movie, "The Peaceful Warrior," is based on the book The Way of the Peaceful Warrior by Dan Millman.[14] It's a true account of a driven young gymnast who is training for Olympic trials. Essentially, he has no interest and no goal beyond Olympic glory. He trains relentlessly and lives furiously for that *future*. Rather predictably, prior to Olympic trials and in a moment of inattention, he has a career ending accident—the result of crashing his motorcycle and crushing a leg bone.

Maimed and angry at the world, Dan begins a downward spiral of self-loathing and destruction. Fortunately, he hooks up with a car mechanic—Socrates, played by a crusty Nick

---

[14] Millman, Dan. The Way of The Peaceful Warrior. CA: HJ Kramer/ New World Library, 2000.

Nolte—who sees his predicament differently and chooses Dan as his "student." In one scene, after Dan complains "nothing's happening around here," his vision and hearing are abruptly hyper-sensitized and he "zooms" into every word, smile, birdsong, gesture and breeze that are occurring within his range. Further compelled by similarly jarring philosophical challenges and questions by his guru, Dan is eventually guided towards peace and astonishing healing.

In the finale, Dan has healed from his injuries and returned to the sport he loved—only now he is experiencing it *moment to moment*. Midway through a difficult routine, he stops and asks himself: "where am I, who am I, what time is it?" He completes the routine flawlessly.

Yesterday, Today or Tomorrow?

What does it mean to live moment to moment and why is it that doing so is so ephemeral? I tend to think there are several reasons:

> We are a goal-oriented culture that celebrates those who drive themselves relentlessly toward a future gain.

> We are an active culture that promotes and rewards the ability to multi-task.

> We're a competitive culture that values a 50-week work-year.

And so forth.

Besides all this, even if we really want to live in the moment, we don't really know how to do so—or even what it means! Well, it means a lot. Whole books on the topic have climbed the bestseller lists year after year. The Power of Now and A New Earth by Ekhart Tolle, Wherever You Go There You Are by Jon

Kabat-Zin, <u>Inner Simplicity</u> by Elaine St. James, just to mention a few.

It's often written that only when we are faced with death, are most of us able to spontaneously convert to living in the now (Remember Ray in chapter 2?). This tells me we have the ability to do so—but not the motivation. For our purposes, what if this ability—to remain in the present—means deeper, more satisfying relationships? What if it means lightening the heavy load of baggage we carry from past grievances? What if it means seeing *what is* more clearly and thus gaining the ability to respond more proactively? What if it means the flow of more inspiration filtering into our lives? Finally, what if it means more moments of unfettered joy in living and *being* with good friends, colleagues and family?

The present moment is underestimated.

The Seagull

Most of us have a challenging relationship with one parent or the other. Mine was with my mom—we are just so different! We frequently have to struggle to maintain emotional balance and appreciation of each other's perspectives. One June, my husband and I planned one of our regular visits to her home in Florida. I decided that no matter what, I wasn't going to live in the past or engage in any testy behavior. In fact, I decided to extend love towards her no matter what transpired. It was a challenge but—from my new position—I saw that she too was anxious about us.

About three days into the visit, the three of us were lying on a beach, all in a row. Mom and I were having a forgettable conversation, when she abruptly burst out in gales of laughter! It was so astonishing to see her belly laugh that I exuberantly joined in. The next moment, with tears in her eyes, she reached into her satchel, pulled out a tissue and began to dab seagull droppings off my visor.

Where were we? There, in that moment of glee.

Who were we? Two people responding to the moment.

What time was it? A magic moment—free of past or future anxiety.

And our relationship began to shift. I can't tell you for sure what transpired in those few moments. But I can surmise. I had decided to operate from a position of only love. To do so, I had to let go of past grievances—on a moment-to-moment basis. My attitude and behavior positively influenced Mom's. And thus …

The universe responded and gave us an opportunity to burst a balloon of past friction. In that healing moment, we embraced the opportunity full throttle. And from that moment forward, she and I have maintained a largely unfettered and loving relationship. Though not always perfect, now we discuss, process and resolve difficult issues. We can "be" together, unencumbered by our turbulent past. In that moment, we gave each other a gift and we're holding on for dear life. A weight has lifted.

I'm grateful that I decided to let go of my past and live each moment with her. This is an example of what it means to "be in the present." The past, after all is over—it's nothing more than a passing breeze. It can only affect me today if I choose to let it do so. And the future is an open book—it can veer in any direction. Why live in fear and dread of it? Why not do what we can to influence it positively, rather than live with the augur of a gloomy foregone conclusion?

The Hourglass

I often lead group meditations. I have a favorite one, in which participants imagine an hourglass perched on the bridge of their nose. It is turned sideways and balanced perfectly with equal amounts of sand in each vessel. The left side is the past. The right side is the future. Slowly but surely the left side tilts down and empties all of one's past. When the left is clear, the right side tilts and empties the future. All that's left is the present. Try it. You will feel the "incredible lightness of being" that living in the moment affords you.

Stop reading at the end of this paragraph. Get a drink of water. Take a few deep breaths. Stretch. Walk around your yard or living space. Retrieve your pen and pad or journal. Record *this moment* by answering such questions as: what do I hear, what do I see, what do I smell, how do I feel? Now become aware of your breathing by following each inhalation and exhalation. Now answer the questions posed at the beginning of the chapter: where are you, who are you, what time is it? Consider what would transpire—or dissolve—if you approached more moments like this.

Chapter 8

The Ecology of Relationship

"The holy relationship is the old unholy relationship transformed and seen anew."
A Course in Miracles[15]

Can you answer the question "who am I?" Can you do so without relying on your roles of family member, ethnicity, professional or hobbyist? E.g., can you describe yourself without the benefit of words such as: son, wife, brother, American, teacher, socialist, environmentalist, writer, Episcopalian, computer analyst, retiree? These, after all, are only titles—they don't reveal an iota of who you *are*. It's not easy to abandon these readily accessible descriptors but I challenge you to do so. How else can you continue your journey towards authenticity? To help you begin, using my husband and myself as examples, I'll give it a go myself.

Who Am I? Who Are You?

I'm an adventurer—the more unfamiliar my surroundings, the more alive I feel. I'm physical—I enjoy activity that

---

15   Schucman, Helen. A Course in Miracles. CA: The Foundation for Inner Peace, 1975.

challenges and strengthens my body. I'm a seeker—I seek new and esoteric knowledge—often just for the fun of it. I'm a nature nymph—I revel in deep interaction with the environment. I'm an individualist—I don't require convention or companionship to feel comfortable. I'm an idea person—I'll conceive of many and complete a few. And so forth.

My husband, on the other hand, is a peace seeker—he'll go to lengths to instill harmony in his environment. He's a doer—he loves initiating and completing projects. He's an aesthetic—he loves to create beauty. He's a keen observer—he can recognize a face or landmark after years of absence. He's an empathizer—he goes out of his way not to hurt others. He's an intuitive—he reads my thoughts. And so forth.

Recognizing your own and others' uniqueness—absent the roles they play in the world—carries you a long way toward the self-acceptance and other-acceptance that generates authentic interaction.

You know by now that my mom and I have healed an historically challenging relationship. Now that you know some of my personality traits, consider this. Mom enjoys structure, security, tradition, conformity and familiarity. She strives to fit in with her surroundings. She's an aesthetic who strives for synchrony and balance in her environment. Though a strong personality, she's very sensitive. She showed love by drawing paper dolls and making clothes for my sisters and me. She was a strict disciplinarian. Our house was neat as a pin. She most approved of my sisters and me when we conformed to family and societal norms and behaved properly.

Are you starting to feel sorry for my mom? Can you imagine trying to raise me to be a "good" girl when my leanings were toward adventure and independence? Yikes! That poor woman. She just wanted me to be a proper member of society. And poor me. I just wanted to go new places, try new things and generally push the envelope—while all the time, I was being reprimanded and grounded for nonconformist behavior. No wonder we were often in conflict.

As a child of any age, it's particularly nice if your parents *parent* you in the way you want to be parented! The problem is …. Well, you know the problem—*we're all different.* For better or worse, we all define love and acceptance differently. My mom—and your mom, for that matter—showed us love the only way they knew how. They had a genetic predisposition to parenting (nature) and a lifetime of experiences affecting their child-rearing decisions and practices (nurture). They did what *they were* and we did what *we were.* God knows I've tried—but I can't judge Mom for her mothering skills—because ya' know what? She was a great mother. And I was a great kid. *We are just different.* And truth be told, I'm probably lucky I didn't have a parent just like me. Can you imagine?

The Flip Side of What We Cherish

Just as my husband is a great husband. I like to tell people that, "I gotta' keep him because he's taken so long to train." But the truth is, we've trained each other. The most valuable lesson we've learned along the way is this; the flip side of what we most cherish is the very thing that drives us nuts. I'll say this in another way. The thing I love most about him is his sensitivity. The thing that drives me up a wall is his sensitivity. The thing he loves most about me is my independence. The thing that drives him up a wall is my independence.

You see, I love it when he's building bookshelves for my office, going to chick-flicks with me, proof-reading my manuscripts or massaging my sore back muscles. On the other hand … I hate it when he chooses not to tell me something unpleasant because he's afraid of hurting my feelings or he drags his feet on a decision because it feels precarious. Essentially, I love his sensitive nature until it collides with my independent nature. My mantras to him are: "Just say it like it is!" "Don't make me guess." "Just do it."

Likewise, he's thrilled when I'm putting myself out there to promote his artwork in new and different ways or I've planned a scenic vacation for us and all he has to do is pack his easel and paints. He loves the parties I plan and the fact that I don't need his presence to have fun or be productive. On the other hand ... he hates it when I involve both of us in some endeavor for which he's not mentally prepared—or if I choose to have a political debate with his father. Ouch. He loves my independent nature until it collides with his sensitive nature. His mantras to me are: "Don't always rock the boat." "Give me a minute to digest this!" "Once in a while, we can do the same thing twice."

I offer these illustrations because they're the ones I know best. As such, they provide the clearest examples of people and their interpersonal challenges. Being human, it's often difficult to look beyond our own thoughts and tendencies when interpreting others' words or a situation. It's no wonder that divorce hovers around the 40 percent mark or that, on average, there are between 40 and 140 wars occurring around the world in any given year. *We don't realize that what we love is what we hate.* And in order to return to love we must recognize—and embrace—this duality. Understanding and embracing this concept is—how shall I say ... hard work!

Stop reading at the end of this paragraph. Get a drink of water. Stretch. Take a few deep breaths. Walk around your yard or living space. Now sit down with pad and paper or journal. Describe yourself without the benefit of roles or titles. For instance: I am an animal lover—my best friends are dogs. I'm a keen competitor—I hate to lose. I'm an over-achiever—I love to excel. And so forth. Stop, rest and return to this later, if you need more time. Now describe a person you're close to in the same fashion. Then consider; what do you love about that person? What drives you nuts? Likewise, what do they love about you and what drives them nuts? Can you discern the commonality between what you love and hate? How does this alter your perceptions? How does this help you to appreciate your attraction and your differences? Take your time, there is no deadline.

Part II

Outer Ecology

"Connecting"

Outer Ecology

"I see you."
Natal Tribes of South Africa

Wow. What a journey. You're lightening your backpack. You're identifying fears, preconceived notions, rigidity and prejudices. You're reassessing the impact of your use of the words "yes" and "no" on your spirit. You're learning to check your ego at the door. You're recalling the stories of your past and assessing their impact on your present. You're learning what it means to live in the now. You're reconsidering the dynamics of a love-hate relationship and re-imagining it to love only. Thank you for your efforts. Your world is opening up and this affects everyone and everything, including me. I do believe that well-intentioned efforts "pay forward."

You do make a difference.

But while you've come a long way, there's more inner and outer work to be done. Your journey, Dear One, is ongoing.

Up until now, you've dealt mainly with your inner ecology. Your knowledge of self has grown and your relationship with self has prospered. Now, you may want to include those around you. You may be ready to be a role model and bring others into the fold. You may be considering interacting differently. It's time to use your newfound inspiration and self-awareness to enhance or revive your outer ecology—through conversation. It's time to connect.

Remember—authentic presence takes courage. It means vocalizing uncertainties and vulnerabilities. It means recognizing that others subscribe to "truths" that are every bit as viable as yours. It means valuing those truths even if you can't agree. It means knowing there are two sides to every story. It means discovering commonality. It means acknowledging the humanity in *everyone*.

The Natal tribes of South Africa embody the spirit of "ubuntu." Essentially, ubuntu means *a person is a person only through others*, e.g., until one is seen, s(he) doesn't exist. As such, tribe members greet each other with the phrase, "sawu bona" which translates as "I see you." The response is "sikhona" translated as "I am here." In other words: *I acknowledge your presence, you have meaning in my world; together we are everything.* How beautiful.

In our Western world, this degree of "otherness" is fundamentally a learned skill. In the chapters that follow, you will not only achieve a greater degree of recognition and appreciation of others who are different from you, you'll discover just how exultant your togetherness can be.

Happy Trails.

Chapter 9

The Ecology of Interaction

"But what do I know?"
the author

There's a reasonably good chance that you want to share your insights, from chapter 8, with someone. That someone might be the person whose personality traits you've been dissecting. I think it's a great idea—and I ask that you tread gently. Remember that not everyone has been digging deep into his or her ecology—or engaging in the degree of self-examination that you have. Not everyone wants to self-analyze or be self-analyzed. Remember, as always, that your conclusions may be *just plain wrong*. No one's interest in—or response to—a situation can be taken for granted. I offer you a personal example.

What Do I Know?

My husband, Kevin is a plein air landscape artist. His paintings are sensitive and soulful. He is committed to interpreting his subject faithful to the scene. Though his style is loose, he doesn't use a lot of artistic license. Unless he runs into an art aficionado on the trail, I'm always the first to see his artwork—just off the easel. I have a preference for highly contrasting values in a painting. So when he asks me what I think of the day's work, I have three general responses.

1. "I love it!" That probably means it's high contrast.
2. "I have to live with it a bit." That means I'm not sure.
3. "I'm not wild about it *but what do I know?*" That means it's probably low contrast. I don't really care for it *and* it'll probably be the <u>first</u> to sell...

You see, we owned an art gallery for several years. Among other things, I was in charge of framing Kevin's work. That also means I selected what was to hang on the walls. I left the rest of the unframed work in a stack in our storage room. In the first year, the walls were filled with the high contrast paintings that I thought were "the best." When someone obviously loved Kevin's work but wasn't finding the perfect match, I would pull out the stack of unframed works. *This is how my lens began to clear.* As often as not, they would select one that I had never even considered for framing—probably because it was subtle or low contrast.

It didn't take long for me to revamp my framing selections to include high and low contrast images. After all, art selection is an emotional decision. And what did I know about what would trigger a positive or negative reaction from a perfect stranger?

And so it is with human interaction. Just as I never knew what genre of artwork would spark an emotional response in a collector, we never know what will spark emotional responses— *positive or negative*—in each other. Some people love to dive into new territory—others are intimidated. Some anticipate and dread confrontation—others thrive on it. Some love to look inward—others run from it.

Personality and/or relationship issues can be thorny. Your words can open doors or have them slammed in your face. The best course—if you're unsure—is simply to clear the path before you tread. So, before sharing your insights from chapter 8, please consider the following examples and advice. Let's say Charlie is your spouse and—through the exercise in chapter 8—you think you've figured out a point of contention in your relationship.

Opening Doors to Understanding

"Charlie—I've been doing some dedicated self-study. It's been grueling and fascinating and surprising at times. Because we're close and I feel we relate well, I've thought about our relationship and have arrived at some interesting thoughts. I'd love to run them by you and hear your response to them. Can we schedule a time to talk?"

Notice ample use of "I." I like the word when introducing a potentially volatile subject. I use it to frame a conversation. It takes the—possibly uncomfortable—focus *off* the recipient. As such, it opens doors of conversation, where use of the—sometimes inflammatory—word "you" often closes them. In contrast, consider the following "bad" example.

Closing Doors to Understanding

"Charlie—I've been miserable for several months now. Everybody thinks we are such a great couple but sometimes you can be so thoughtless, I think you're in another world. Other times, you hold everything in and then you blow up like a balloon. I've been reading this book and I think I know why you can push my buttons so. I need to discuss it as soon as possible."

Poor Charlie. Even if he wanted to have a civil conversation, he's heard the accusatory "you" so many times that he's probably beyond civility. He's been judged and he's likely feeling pretty darned defensive. The door to heartfelt conversation was partially, if not fully closed from the get-go. Good luck getting his attention.

Here are some additional guidelines for addressing potential tough stuff.

Addressing the Tough Stuff

1. Remember your affection for the person you're addressing.
2. If you're feeling hesitancy to express yourself, say so. E.g. "I want to talk about something and I'm feeling a little scared about it. Can you bear with me?" Silence.
3. Relate what you want to talk about. E.g. "I'd like to talk about some rough spots in our relationship. It means so much to me and I just want to seek some clarity. OK?" Silence.
4. Be specific. E.g. "Sometimes I feel you withdrawing. I'm pretty sure something is upsetting you but I don't know what. I just feel if we bit the bullet and talked about it sooner, rather than later it wouldn't escalate like it sometimes does. We're both so miserable afterwards." Silence.
5. Stay on topic. If you find yourselves branching off into unrelated territory, simply request that you return to the original conversation. E.g. "That's important too, but can we return to the original question and address this later?"
6. Remember, there are two sides to every story. Listen to, and consider the other side.
7. When you've reached agreement, suggest a protocol for staying the course. E.g. "So if we revert to our old behavior, shall we give each other the thumbs down sign?"
8. Recall your affection for the person you've just addressed. Express it along with your gratitude.

Kevin and I have a saying when disagreements get out of hand. We just yell, "Shut your pie hole!" Then the other responds "No, you shut you're pie hole!" I've even been known to say it to myself. It's a line delivered by Jack Nicholson's character in the movie, "Anger Management." It's just so outrageous, that we both bust out laughing—no matter how mad we are. Then we're able to get back on track. Laughter is a panacea. You're welcome to borrow our phrase—particularly if you've seen the movie and had a similar reaction!

Having agreement on a non-threatening way of returning to balance is very helpful and affirming.

Stop reading at the end of this paragraph. Get a drink of scotch (Oops! Did I say that? Of course, I meant water). Stretch. Take a few deep breaths. Walk around your yard or living space. Retrieve your pen and pad or journal. Now write down what you want to say and to whom. Compose your text and practice your tone and words with someone neutral. Take your time. With purity of spirit, an open heart—and recognizing that you may be wrong about some things—share your discoveries with this person. Then listen; really listen to what s/he has to say. There's a good chance you'll learn something.

Chapter 10

The Ecology of Listening

"It's a rare person who wants to hear what he doesn't want to hear."
Dick Cavett (TV personality)

Until now, we haven't directly addressed the art of listening. Listening is kind of like the air we breathe. Sometimes it's fresh and clear and unpolluted. Like a mountain vista, it renews, refreshes and nourishes every cell of our bodies. We're often not even aware of it and yet it rewards us with health, well-being and vitality. But sometimes, clear air is filled with invisible pollutants—like when I lived in a high technology corridor. The air looked clear but a cough here or a runny nose there caused subtle but chronic discomfort. It became so "normal" that I didn't even notice its unhealthy effects. Occasionally air is just plain murky and smelly and its source is evident—like a malodorous smokestack. We don't have to wonder, we remove ourselves from its toxicity ASAP.

Fresh Air

And so it is with listening. Uninterrupted and empathetic listening is like a breath of fresh, clean air. It nourishes and warms the recipient—adding to one's health and well-being. While obvious disrespect and disregard, by the listener, causes one to retreat and shut down—just like fleeing a stinky smokestack. It's that *in-between state*—that looks like listening but is characterized by selective attention, cursory feedback, or a rush to conclusion— that is most toxic. It's become so common that we often fail to recognize its cumulative effects, not only in interpersonal and business relationships, but also on the human spirit. We just sense that we're beginning to disappear.

In the previous pages we've been "listening" to our own inner words, stories and reactions. We've been delving into their history, content and meaning. We've made strides in recognizing their influence on us—and our subsequent interpretations of others' words and stories. We've begun to free ourselves of automatic reactions and snap judgments. The air is clearing, as we begin to know ourselves better through inner listening and attention.

Now it is time to use that clarity to listen to others, as well. "Oh My!" you may be thinking. It was really hard work getting to this point. Do I have to start all over again? The answer is yes and no. Yes, to complete this journey, you must begin to attend to others as well as yourself. And no—it shouldn't be so arduous. For you've learned the basic skills already. Now all you have to do is transfer them to your *outer* ecology.

Deep Listening—It's Contagious

It's easier than you think. Remember Ray (from chapter 2) and the truth fests? Remember his vulnerability and authentic presence? Truth telling and receiving is contagious. Often times all it takes is one person to courageously reveal his or her inner workings for others to follow suit. When the truth is spoken, *more people listen!* When half-truths are spoken, more people drift off. It's a virtuous cycle or a vicious cycle. If one person is willing to be a role model for truth telling, together with *deep listening*— the air eventually clears. And it begins to circulate in soft healing breezes that feed the spirits of the whole. This takes courage! But the subsequent sharing of life, love and information generate the mutually enriching conversations that we've been seeking. This is the gift we give to others and ourselves.

To get you started, here are some of the deep listening concepts you will want to embrace and role model, together with inspirational *mantras*.

> Stillness—I'm quiet in mind and body. Thus I pay better attention.
> Dedication to the message—I hear the content of the message in its entirety.
> Reflection and inquiry—I think I'm hearing this. Am I correct? I ask.
> Beginner's Mind—I have something to learn.
> Presence—I am here and now 100 percent.

The First Meeting

I worked with the Executive Directors—a man and a woman—of two nonprofit agencies who served the same population. I'll call them Sam and Sue. Since they were in the same city, their boards determined that it would be in everyone's best interest if the two collaborated on a regular basis. But, there was a problem. The two harbored a longstanding, embedded disdain for each other. They avoided each other like the plague. It goes without saying that this presented a huge stumbling block—not only to the boards' wishes but also to the populations they served. I was hired to figure out what the problem was and help them reach an alliance.

It was a fascinating intervention. The two couldn't have been more similar if they were raised in the same family. Both were well educated with the same advanced degree, had the same religious affiliation, similar parentage (both had a parent who was clergy), they even cited the same role model and hero—Albert Schweitzer—who influenced their life's work. In every way, they *should* have been completely compatible.

For several weeks—an hour here, an hour there, I worked with each individually. I wanted to hear their stories. Ultimately, I realized that in their very *first* meeting, they had totally misinterpreted something that was spoken between them. Not uncommon in our workplaces—a gender issue had reared its perplexing head. In the words that were spoken (whatever they were), Sue thought Sam was propositioning her. Sam—who had been in the field longer—thought he was simply offering collegial support of Sue's new position and agency. Sue withdrew. Sam was offended. Rather than checking for clarification both took offense and maintained this stubborn Mexican standoff for the ensuing years.

When I brought them together—in an understandably prickly setting—and this misunderstanding was finally made transparent, they were shell-shocked and frankly, disbelieving. Silence prevailed as they digested this new information. Their working relationship improved greatly—but truth be told, I'm not sure they ever reached *total* acceptance—the sentiment had become so ingrained that it was almost cellular in its toxicity.

Consider everyone who was hurt or underserved because of this attachment to message. Sam and Sue hurt themselves because their boards thought less of them for not collaborating—and they lived with the polluting effects of unresolved anger and resentment. They hurt their staffs because they weren't able to contribute fully to their agencies or community. They hurt their community because their "customers" were underserved. In one moment, two agencies became less than they could or should have been. Sadly, this genre of misunderstanding—a simple matter of poor listening and inquiry—runs rampant in our world. It's tragic. It's daunting. The remedy requires some reassessment of what it means to be fully present. More on this in Chapter 11.

Commitment to listening is akin to meditation. It means securing yourself in the present moment in order to focus on the person and/or the conversation entirely. It means diverting incoming thoughts so you don't edit or misinterpret the words of others. It means seeking clarification if you're unsure. It means faith in an outcome that is—as yet—unknown. When I achieve this degree of concentration, I feel peaceful and focused—just like I do in meditation. Had Sam and Sue engaged—if only partially—in this behavior, their history would've been all together different.

Stop reading at the end of this paragraph. Get a drink of water. Stretch. Take a few deep breaths. Walk around your yard or living space. Retrieve your pen and pad or journal. Describe the feeling you have when you know you're being seen and heard. E.g., I feel accepted. I feel important. Now recall the feeling you get when you've had a conversation, rich in sharing and receiving of unpolluted information. E.g., I feel inspired. I feel connected.

Put those feelings on paper. Set one listening goal for the next time you're part of a conversation or meeting. For best results use, first person, present tense, positive terms—as I did under "concepts." For example, "When I find my mind drifting, I return immediately to full attention" or "I am a compassionate listener." Write it down. Share it with someone. Remember, pure, unfettered communication is contagious. You're becoming a role model for others.

Chapter 11

The Ecology of Mental Clutter

"Clearing clutter in all forms allows our original purpose in coming here to resurface and shine through. This brings with it immense clarity and a profound sense of knowing what to do."
Karen Kingston, Clear Your Clutter With Feng Shui[16]

How do Sam and Sue begin to untangle and dislodge all of those misfired neurons—embedded in their brains after years of operating on misinformation? How do they clear the mental clutter of ingrained assumptions that are no longer valid? Don't assume they can pick up from that meeting and say "Whew! I'm glad that's over with! Let's go on as if nothing happened." Nope, not even close. Over the years, words were spoken or not, actions were taken or not, feelings were felt intensely. Reverberations occurred on many levels. Some issues still had to be addressed.

If you're a heart-based person, you're probably experiencing palpable discomfort for these two right now. If you're a head-based person, you're probably marveling at the convolution of the human condition. How do we humans turn something so

---

[16]   Kingston, Karen. Clear Your Clutter With Feng Shui. NY: Broadway Books, 1999.

ephemeral—as passing words—into such a web of intrigue? While the ecology of the human spirit is often resilient beyond comprehension, it can also be inexplicably fragile.

My Office

I have a small, irregularly shaped home office. Bookshelves line the walls and there are two chairs wedged into the corners of the space. My desk and chair take up about 35 percent of the room. At least once a month, my desktop gets so full of extraneous stuff that I'll make stacks and transfer them to the chairs. Back to work I go. Shortly the piles reappear and—with nowhere to transfer them—my brain rebels, my writing becomes labored and my pulse begins to race. Believe me when I tell you that my body's electrical charge can become so erratic that my computer will *frequently* malfunction at this point! I have no choice but to attend to each and every item on my desk and chairs—filing, discarding, sending or placing them in a "to do" stack.

Occasionally, I deem myself too busy for this annoying detail work. I exit my office, close the door, retrieve my laptop and transfer everything I'm working on to the kitchen table—thus escaping the clutter. Oh, I'm so smart. But you guessed it— suddenly a civilized breakfast for either my husband or me—is utterly hopeless. Now I'm agitated in two rooms of my home! Once, I even left that mess and moved to the game table in our sunroom. When it filled up, I considered, and then rejected the idea of moving to the public library. What a complete and total ecological disaster! I had to retrace my steps and attend to three gruelingly chaotic workspaces. Oh, how I wished I'd simply addressed the clutter issue in the first place—and space.

Mental and Emotional Clutter

And so it is with human interactions. We perceive a slight, we take offense, we assume our interpretation is true; we operate on this information—sometimes for years. When we don't make a habit of fact or feeling checks, our assumptions are frequently incomplete or just plain wrong. When we finally get an inkling that something just isn't matching up, we're so invested in the emotions of it all that it's difficult to conceive of ever making things right again. Moving out of town would be easier!

Sam and Sue's brains were so full of years of mental and emotional clutter, that it would take real effort and self-possession to clear it completely. But fortunately, the desire for that delicious feeling of letting go—that often accompanies forgiveness—can be strong. And reaching understanding can be revelatory. Like others who have been misinformed or misguided, I recommended they spend some times together—either over a bottle of wine or pot of tea—to reconstruct those memories. In addition to abundant use of the word "I"—as we discussed in chapter 9—I suggested they engage in open-ended questioning, accompanied by deep listening, reflection and inquiry.

Open-ended Questioning

Open-ended questions are generative in any setting—not just while in conflict. Yet many haven't a clue what an open-ended question is. It is one whose purpose is to achieve clarity or insight, *not* confirmation of one's own beliefs. It is therefore stated in such a way that its content is not burdened with the questioner's point of view. The response is subsequently untainted by the influence or motive of the questioner. For example,

> "Sam, remember that city council meeting we both attended last June—the one where they were discussing ordinance 77.77? What was your interpretation of their decision and how did you follow through on it?"

> "Sue, remember when you spoke at that conference in Seattle? You were so passionate on the passage of

Issue 8. What fuels your passion for this issue? And how do you incorporate it into your agency's work?"

"Remember when we both responded to that shortage of resources in 2003? You were quoted on the front page of the newspaper. I never understood the reasoning behind your response. Can you help me to understand?"

"What's the most rewarding aspect of your job?"

Open-ended questions, like these, are for the sole purpose of illumination. Relaxing into the response—in other words, listening with generosity of spirit and a desire to understand—can be such an uplifting experience! But our ego doesn't want us to know this. Ego exerts a strong current of defense—when there's a chance that we might just be wrong. It struggles so hard to confirm existing beliefs, that it frequently prevents us from hearing that which might uplift and illuminate. Such a sadistic cycle!

Reflection and Inquiry

The communication skills of "reflection and inquiry" are one's best defense against falling prey to the ego's desire for affirmation. Reflection—sometimes called "mirroring"—is as it sounds: someone speaks to you and you reflect back what you've heard. Inquiry is also as it sounds—you simply ask for confirmation that you heard the message accurately. For example,

Sam—The most rewarding aspect of my job is knowing that I'm helping people in need.

Sue—You love to help people on the street. I do too.

Sam—Well, yes and no. I love creating programs that help them. But I also include my staff in this sentiment. Most people who work for nonprofits have some sort of history of poverty or abuse. I believe they feel the need to give back, in order to heal themselves.

Sue—So you enjoy leading your staff.

Sam—Well, not really. Managing people is a pain in the butt. If I had my druthers, I'd have an assistant who dealt with the people issues.

Sue—So what I'm hearing is: you like the "big picture" aspect of helping people in need. You like to create an environment for helping. You like to manage the projects. You're fulfilled by the outcome. Right?

Sam—Right!

And so forth! Reflecting a person's words confirms what you've heard—or not. It encourages expansion of a concept, together with deeper understanding. Inquiry checks for accuracy and agreement—and prevents misinterpretation. Deep listening does take time and effort. But in the long run, it saves time and effort.

Closed-end Questioning

The opposite of open-ended questioning is characterized by the stereotypical courtroom drama. The questioner strives to generate a short, pre-determined, useful response. For example:

"Were you or were you not a witness to the accident? Yes or no?"

"When did you become friends with the defendant? 2008 or 2009?"

"What was your recommendation to the board? To extend my client's contract or to fire him?"

"Why did you sexually harass my client?"

EEK! My heart races just envisioning these scenarios. Talk about stacking clutter on top of clutter. What if you heard the accident and then turned to it, missing the actual stimulus? What if you were friendly, but not a friend of the subject? What if you recommended extending the contract if the person would accept counseling? What if you never harassed the client? Closed-end questioning does the opposite of open-ended—it invites misunderstanding. It keeps us safely within our own self-imposed boundaries of reality. *It's expedient.* The ego—which guards our sense-of-self come hell or high water—doesn't have to stretch.

Let's get back with Sam and Sue. Like them, sometimes we are so invested in our own interpretation of a situation that every subsequent word or event fuels the last, creating even more justification for misguided feelings. The act of going back and sifting through the piles of debris can seem daunting—*but not so time consuming as you might imagine.*

You see, once you leave your ego at the door and jump into heartfelt communication, things begin to fall into place. Patterns emerge, hurt feelings heal and there is no longer need to revisit every *single slight.* Forgiveness and understanding often receive enough illumination to bloom after clearing the air on a few core issues.

In the case of Sam and Sue, the core issue for Sue is whether Sam treats her with respect, not condescension. The core issue for Sam is whether Sue is willing to collaborate on projects without misinterpreting his words. Both need to embrace th roles they played in the original misunderstanding and commit to not repeating a similar outcome.

There are *always* two sides to every story.

Stop reading at the end of this paragraph. Get a drink of water. Stretch. Take a few deep breaths. Walk around your yard or living space. Retrieve your pen and pad or journal. Recall a longstanding misunderstanding that you would really like to deconstruct. For example, "my neighbor and I disagree on tree-trimming issues on our property line." Consider the core issue(s) surrounding the misunderstanding. For example, "she wants to cut, I want to trim." Take time with this consideration, because it's likely that your first thought is actually *a symptom* of the core issue. For example, the *core issue* here may actually be: you like to forage for nuts; she doesn't like the little seedlings that crop up every spring. To arrive at the core issue, compose three open-ended questions, the answers to which would help you to understand and address the situation better. For example: why do you favor cutting down the trees; why are the trees bothersome; if we work together, will you consider alternatives to cutting?

Now position two chairs in a face-off position, a few feet apart. One chair holds you, the other chair "holds" the person you'd like to address. Sit in your chair and ask your first question of the other chair. Now change positions; *assume the viewpoint of the other*, and respond, as you believe they would if they were to speak from their heart. *Listen to their heart with your heart.* Repeat the process until you've asked your questions and have received answers. If other questions arise, continue. You're now ready to do this in real time.

Bon Chance!

Chapter 12

The Ecology of Community

"The peace we seek is found in experiencing ourselves as part of something bigger and wiser than our little, crazed self."
Margaret Wheatley, <u>Turning to One Another</u>[17]

Solitude or Community?

Our interactions with others are one of our most precious gifts. They rank right up there with the air we breathe and the water we drink. Without a history of a parent's touch, family's words, membership in groups—or some facsimiles thereof—we live a solitary, if not wretched existence. Our lives are so enriched by interactions with others—and yet we are steadily moving toward a society of increasing solitude and loneliness.

We move away from family. We marry and bear children later—and have fewer of them. We telecommute. We email, Google or text instead of call. We go to work early and come

---

[17]   Reprinted with permission of the publisher. <u>Turning to One Another</u> ©2002,Margaret Wheatley, (Berrett-Koehler Publishers, Inc. San Francisco, CA) All rights reserved. www.bkconnection.com.

home late. We skip vacations with our families. It's no wonder that a quarter of Americans queried admit the absence of a close confidante in their lives—a figure that has doubled in just twenty years (Maggie Jackson, <u>Distracted</u>, p. 22).[18]

I often hear some of my better-traveled friends proclaim sympathy for those in lesser-developed countries. They comment on small or poorly constructed homes, lack of air conditioning, inadequate transportation or technology, etc.

> "In the Eastern bloc they still plow their fields with horses!"
> "In Central America they live in block structures, without doors or windows!"
> "In Asia, several generations live under one roof."

And so forth.

I'm not naïve—I know we, in the West, have it so easy compared to third-world countries—and for this I'm grateful. But nonetheless, these comments frequently send me off into daydreams themed "less is more." In those dreams, I imagine the breeze flowing through my room as I sleep, a day spent guiding a Clydesdale up and down rows of corn, a ready-made group of loved ones to chew the fat with anytime. Realistic or not, these imaginings soothe me. I've often envied those with fewer choices, less noise, more contact with nature and so on.

I know this will make me sound old. Having spanned the decades from the 1950's through today, I have the misfortune of memories of more frequent and poignant interactions—not only with people, but also with animals and nature. I miss interacting with people whose jobs are now obsolete: librarians, telephone operators, secretaries, customer service representatives and street sweepers! I miss exploratory days spent outside and returning for

---

[18]   Jackson, Maggie. <u>Distracted</u>. NY: Prometheus Books, 2008.

dinner sunburned and bee-stung. I miss open windows where the breeze, butterflies and pollen float in one and out the other. I miss the days of limited choices! I miss neighborhoods with people on the streets, sidewalks and yards. I miss single-tasking. But more than anything, I feel sorry for those who will never know the difference.

Executive Dinner Forum

As human systems consultant to Fortune and International 500 companies, I've witnessed this deterioration of human and environmental interaction in the business ecosystem. It started as a whisper back in the early 80's and has progressed to a roar today.

In the early 80's, the teams I worked with were still bright-eyed and eager to work together toward common goals. They were friends as well as colleagues. Then little by little, morale diminished with the effects of downsizing, mergers, outsourcing, acquisitions, globalization, teleconferencing, telecommuting, PowerPoint, email, blackberry and text ... Egad! Gone was job security and company loyalty—followed by insurance plans, pensions, integrity and commitment. Work is largely a mechanism today—as opposed to a way of life.

In the 1990's—as a response to the trends I was observing—I formed and facilitated Executive Dinner Forum (EDF). I did so because I recognized a pattern of heart-rending isolation at the top of organizations, too. Not only were high level executives isolated from their subordinates, the competition was often so thick within their ranks, that they had few to confide in across organizational charts. Many high level executives had lost their excitement and sparkle. This isolation left them, their companies—and their employees—vulnerable.

So, I invited several top-level clients from different companies and industries to meet once a month for dinner and conversation. Eight committed. What followed was one of the most satisfying interludes of my career—and hopefully theirs', as well. Eac month a different member chose a topic of conversation. That member and I would meet several weeks before to identify the desired direction of the conversation, choose reading material and select one to three questions to pose to the group. We embraced specific guidelines for "dialogue" (see chapters 13 and 15). My job as facilitator was simply to provide structure, role model dialogue and keep them on track.

Our evenings began at 6:00 with wine and appetizers. Shortly, we would introduce the topic and ask for initial feedback from each member. Dinner followed and usually included further exploration of the topic. After dinner, we delved deeply into the "questions." Finally, we concluded the evening—around 10:00— with "a-ha's" and individual feedback for the featured member.

In the first year, we met in various members' boardrooms with a catered meal. Later, we began meeting in my home around my kitchen island, dining room table and living room. Conversations evolved from strictly business in the first years, to pointedly personal in the remaining years. Essentially, members wanted to become more self-aware—through the reflections of those they trusted.

EDF lasted for five years until my husband and I moved from the area. As the time of my departure approached, the group became more determined to achieve the most possible gain, both individually and collectively. As such, we spent the last three months on a self-awareness instrument called the Enneagram. This instrument is not a quick fix like others on the market (the DISC, Myers Briggs, FIRO B to mention a few). Rather, if allowed, it punctures one's veneer and navigates to the core of one's vulnerabilities. This was a huge step for these strong, accomplished executive types. But five years later they were comfortable in their own—and each others' skins.

I miss these guys. When I moved, I was determined to remain "connected," so I proposed a virtual EDF. Predictably, that didn't fly. Virtual lacked too much of what we had built: spontaneity, warmth, camaraderie, and physical presence. Some have retired.

Others have started their own businesses. Others have moved to the top of organizations.

This degree of camaraderie is a rarity in today's business arena. And truth be told, it's a shame that a facilitator was required for them—or any group—to reach this degree of intimacy. Nonetheless, my belief is they are making a major difference today as a result of their dedicated commitment to themselves, each other and Executive Dinner Forum.

Stop reading at the end of this paragraph. Get a drink of water. Stretch. Take a few deep breaths. Walk around your yard or living space. Retrieve your pen and pad or journal. Recall groups of which you've been a part. Consider the qualities and characteristics of those that really clicked. List them. What role did you play? How did the group achieve balance and equality? What were the struggles? How was conflict resolved? Take notes of your thoughts.

Chapter 13

The Ecology of Meaning

*"Out beyond ideas of wrongdoing and rightdoing, there is a field.
I will meet you there."*
Rumi

How did Executive Dinner Forum arrive at this level of comfort?

The Chaos Theory

It all began with the Chaos Theory. A few years earlier, I had attended a daylong workshop on the subject. As is my pattern, I did so strictly on faith. I had no idea what this so-called theory was or what to expect from the day. I liked the guy who organized it and I was curious. The workshop proved interesting to say the least.

Based on the Chaos principal of "self-organizing systems," (the tenet that we can't *make* anything happen, we can only influence an outcome), there was no agenda whatsoever. The day progressed ever so slowly, with most of us wandering around wondering what we were supposed to be doing! Being a nature nymph, I finally wandered outside and began playing in a sandbox. Eventually another woman—a freelance writer—joined me; she was equally mystified. So, there we sat exchanging pleasantries, sifting through sand and discovering commonalities. Little did we know the system was indeed self-organizing. Years later she joined the Executive Dinner Forum and later, helped to propel my avocation as a writer. But, I digress.

The day ended uneventfully and unceremoniously. Yet, my curiosity had been piqued. I bought books on chaos and team leadership—since this was my field. Over time, I integrated the chaos theory into my work with corporations.

Part and parcel to the study of chaos is a principal of conversation called "dialogue." Physicist, David Bohm—together with Donald Factor and Peter Garrett—first adapted the concept in 1983. The purpose of dialogue is to create access to a "field" of meaning surrounding a group or topic. It is assumed that the field contains not only the people—but also the palpable connections between them. As such, the field contains all the available knowledge, skills and information one might want or need to achieve mastery of a subject or initiative. This thought of having everything at my fingertips is exhilarating. The goal then, is to create an environment where those connections are fully realized. The intended outcome of such interaction is called *group mastery*. (Peter Senge, The Fifth Discipline)[19] More about this later.

Prior to this time, I'd amply employed the practice of "brainstorming" with groups with whom I was working. The two—dialogue and brainstorming—appear similar. Both are an active vocalization of information. But dialogue advances the process and evolves the outcomes. Whereas, the purpose of brainstorming is to put everyone's thoughts and ideas out there, the purpose of dialogue is to create *new meaning*. I get chills just thinking about it.

---

[19]   Senge, Peter. The Fifth Discipline. NY: Doubleday Curren« 1990.

Judith Beck, M.A.

Creating New Meaning

You see—brainstorming is easy. It asks nothing of the participant other than the contribution of an insight, opinion, fact or lie—for that matter. The cream seldom rises to the top in a typical brainstorm session. Dialogue, however, is not easy. In fact, it's downright challenging. But, I've been told that nothing *good* comes easily and I do believe this. Conditions for dialogue, as identified by David Bohm are:

1. Participants must "suspend" assumptions, literally to hold them "as if suspended before us."
2. Participants must regard each other as colleagues.
3. There must be a facilitator who "holds the context" of dialogue.

Theoretically, numbers 2 and 3 are easy and require little explanation. But it takes a special group who is proficient at 1 to succeed at 2. That's where a self-aware leader, accompanied by a skilled facilitator, comes in handy. This being said, the suspension of assumptions is the key to creating *new* meaning.

Suspending one's assumptions means releasing one's hold on that which one assumes to be true, thus creating room for additional information. Enough people in a dialogue must be acquainted with this in order for dialogue to reap rewards. When this is so, group interaction can become, not only educational and informative, but also delightfully playful. The ecosystem blooms and thrives. You, my savvy dears, have been practicing suspending your assumptions (about self and others) for 13 chapters now. Voila! You are ready to move to the next square.

As a reminder, your assumptions are those conditioned thoughts, feelings, prejudices, snap-decisions and inclinations that you've been re-examining and filtering in the previous chapters. Suspending them means recognizing their subjective nature and even vocalizing them as subjective opinions. From them, you've come to realize that just because you *know* something, it doesn't make it so. You've recognized that we are all different and subsequently define the world around us differently. What's true and right for you is entirely subjective—for truth comes in all varieties, shapes and forms. Accepting and appreciating this, embracing the value of a larger truth, committing to the loving act of giving and receiving "truth"—that's what these pages are all about.

Stop reading at the end of this paragraph. Get a drink of water. Stretch. Take a few deep breaths. Walk around your yard or living space. Retrieve pen and pad or journal. Imagine for a moment how your world might expand by involvement in unpolluted dialogue. Play with the concept without edit, fear, self-criticism or judgment. Let your thoughts flow freely. How do you feel? Are you ready to proceed? Write down ways in which you might benefit. Formulate and record some goals. For example, I'll form more substantive relationships, I'll improve my conversational skills, I'll gain self-confidence. I'll learn new things.

Chapter 14

The Ecology of Dialogue

"... collectively, we can be more insightful, more intelligent than we can possibly be individually. The IQ of the team can, potentially, be much greater than the IQ of the individuals."
Peter Senge, The Fifth Discipline[20]

So what exactly does dialogue look like? I will tell you from my own experience.

Checking In

Dialogue looks like a group of people convened in a space, with no apparent leadership position. These people have agreed on a topic. A facilitator calls the meeting to order and each individual "checks in." Checking in involves answering the question "what is influencing my presence at the meeting today?" For instance, you may be on top of the world due to the successful completion of a major project. You may have been up half the night with a sick child. You may be awaiting notice of a promotion, etc. Checking in allows you and others to recognize—and then set aside that which may be competing

[20]   Senge, Peter. The Fifth Discipline. NY: Doubleday Currency, 1990.

for attention. It also promotes an atmosphere of tolerance and understanding. You now appreciate a bit of fatigue from Sue, heightened anxiety from Phil, some unusual exuberance from Robin.

The facilitator introduces the topic and opens the floor for initial sentiments. In the early stages of dialogue, going around the room and hearing from everyone sequentially can set the stage for robust conversation. There are always enlightening surprises (like when Sarah, from chapter 3, proclaimed she could never feel completely secure). It is also OK "to pass." It's frequently advisable to repeat this circuit to tap the well of information even further. Those who passed in the first round have been stimulated and are frequently ready to contribute.

It's important to remember that we all have our own style of processing information. Introverts process information in their heads. That's why they wait a moment before speaking. They're thinking about what they want to say. By contrast, extroverts process information in the outer world – that's why you hear them "thinking out loud." The group gains access to their thought processes—not so with introverts. Without the circuit, the pendulum may tilt toward extroverts who are putting the information "out there" so they can process—and thus convey their real message. They may inadvertently fill the available air space. Both introverts and extroverts reach a conclusion at the same rate—you're just not privy to the introvert's reasoning processes. For this reason, in the spirit of dialogue, moments of silence are golden. Indeed sometimes, throughout the dialogue, it is good to simply mandate silence—for people, extroverts and introverts alike—to gather their thoughts.

The Field

Following these rather structured initial processes, the group is free to contribute at will. This is a time for exploration and discovery—a blossoming, if you will. Being human, it is easy to get off track or carried away, however. The role of the facilitator is to promote and preserve a nourishing "ecosystem." S/he does so by observing and listening intently for signs that the group may be straying or that someone is dominating or holding back. Just as importantly, the facilitator may gently challenge anyone who may be exhibiting rigidity or judgment—thus inhibiting the flow of information and conversation. True to the spirit of dialogue, participants are also encouraged to voice their observations of the process flow.

Participants' role, in addition to contributing freely, is to maintain a beginner's mind—both in giving and receiving of information—and to *speak their truth without negating the truth of others.* This can be tough. After all, we're taught debate in school, not dialogue. So, the skill set requires practice, discipline and dedication. Different groups I've interacted with—and dialogue centers around the world—have developed individualized guidelines in support of these skills. I'll share some of them with you in the next chapter.

Wrapping It Up

The dialogue must end sometime! Generally, time periods are specified for the various segments of the session, for example: check-in—15 minutes; dialogue—1 and 1/2 hours; wrap up—15 minutes. In wrap up, participants may be asked to synthesize what they've learned or voice their conclusions. Or they may be asked for an "a'ha" moment—or how they want to proceed from here. Content of the final commentary depends on the desired outcome of the group. So, there is no standard. But, this is the phase of the dialogue where it is OK—even encouraged—to condense information and draw a conclusion. The reason? If the dialogue has gone as planned, the group has sowed information and discovered new meaning. They've acquired a heightened IQ on the subject matter—the result of listening, contributing, questioning and maintaining a beginner's mind. No matter any individual's opinion at this point, it is based on a higher realm of seeking and knowing. *This is the ideal of dialogue.*

At this point, if the group is still learning to dialogue, it's a good idea to ask of them: how did we do? What skills have we mastered? What still needs work? How can we do even better next time? How can we create even more new meaning?

Finally, while the facilitator should remain objective during the process, I believe it's OK for her to summarize at this point—with the consent of the group. I have found that groups want to know how they are doing. This is a great time to role model dialogue behavior and feedback.

As structured as this may appear, when placed on paper in neat little paragraphs, I have yet to facilitate a group that is not developing its own rhythm and standards for excellence. Dialogue, when thoughtfully executed, requires little facilitation and brings out the best in people. It's beautiful. It's tender. It's frequently revelatory.

Stop reading at the end of this paragraph. Get a drink of water. Stretch. Take a few deep breaths. Walk around your yard or living space. Retrieve pen and pad or journal. Take a good look *inside yourself*. Write down the answers to these questions. What skills do I need to acquire to become proficient at dialogue? What skills can I presently role model? What fears do I have around acquisition or exposure of these skills? Be candid. This is for your consideration only.

Chapter 15

The Ecology of Love

"Be there, speak the truth, let go of the outcome."
(Commonly attributed to Native American Circles)

There are all kinds of dialogue groups—formed and forming—all around the country and the world. We, as a culture, seem to be achieving a growing collective unconsciousness that draws us toward one another again. I don't believe this is just wishful thinking. We've experienced and have tired of this culture of speed—and now we are ready to return to love.

Speed or Love?

From the early to mid 90's, I went to graduate school nights while working fulltime as a human systems consultant days. So by day, I was observing and addressing the stresses of people just trying to keep up with the accelerating and often dehumanizing pace of change in their work lives. At night, I was intellectualizing it in the classroom.

One evening, my professor asked the class—what is the most pressing business issue of the day? Mind you, most of the students were working professionals. After some silence, two of us raised our hands at once. He called on my classmate—

who coincidentally worked for one of my clients, a global telecommunications giant. She declared that "speed" was the most pressing issue of the day. Then he turned to me. I declared that it was "love." No one knew quite what to make of this duality. But suffice to say that a spirited exchange followed, with classmates frequently chiming in.

Coming from our differing perspectives, we were both right. For in order to survive the global competition for telecommunications supremacy, employees felt they had to engage in a continual race for the best technology. And *that* technology *also* had to be fast. Whoever arrived first won. And then the race began all over again.

I saw this unrelenting contest leaving employees drained, their resilience sapped. So from my perspective, I believed that in order to win the race, employees had to be treated humanely. In my mind, love had to precede speed for employees to do their best—and thus win the race. It was a discussion of what comes first—the chicken or the egg. Though we understood each other's perspective, neither of us could divert from our positions. I guess our jobs depended on it!

I love dialogues like this—ones that leave all involved stimulated and enlightened. From its core, dialogue is, indeed, a model for love. For it to succeed, participants must recognize the value of each person's perspective. They must demonstrate that belief through generous and heartfelt interactions. To value and be valued, after all, is at the core of our humanity.

Lucky you. You have done the hard work that readies you for genuine participation in dialogue. Presuming you're contemplating joining or forming a dialogue group, you have the opportunity to contribute to the creation of protocol that guides your interactions with one another. Guidelines are generated by the group and thus will differ, based on the purpose and composition of that group. To wrap your head around this idea, I offer a few of the formulas—some condensed for brevity—

from the many and varied groups that have evolved from David Bohm's—and others'—original "conditions for dialogue."

Formulas for Dialogue

The World Café (www.theworldcafe.com)—an online resource for forming groups who engage in "conversations that matter."

Set the context.
Create hospitable space.
Explore questions that matter.
Encourage everyone's contribution.
Connect diverse perspectives.
Listen together for insights.
Share collective discoveries.

The Wisdom Circle (www.wisdomcircle.org)—an online resource for forming groups interested in "self-discovery and community building."

Honor the circle as sacred time and space by doing simple rituals to mark the beginning and end of conversation.
Create a collective center by mutually agreeing upon a topic or intention.
Ask to be informed by our highest human values such as compassion and truth.
Express gratitude for the blessing and teachings of life.
Acknowledge and honor our interdependence with everything in the web of life.
Create a container for full participation and deep truth-telling.
Allow each person to speak without interruption or cross-talk.
Listen from the heart and serve as compassionate witness—not fixer—to other people in the group.

National Coalition for Dialogue and Deliberation (www. thataway.org)—an online resource for "fostering a world of conversation, participation and action."

Listen carefully and with respect.
One person speaks at a time.
Speak for yourself and not for the group.
Seek to understand rather than persuade.

Sacred Circle (Julia Cameron, The Artist's Way)—guidelines for groups who are following exercises in the book.

Creativity flourishes in a place of safety and acceptance.
Creativity grows among friends, withers among enemies.
All creative ideas are children who deserve our protection.
All creative success requires creative failure.
Fulfilling our creativity is a sacred trust.
Violating someone's creativity violates a sacred trust.
Creative feedback must support the creative child, never shame it.
Creative feedback must build on strengths, never focus on weakness.
Success occurs in clusters and is born in generosity.
The good of another can never block our own.

Society for Philosophical Inquiry (www.philosopher.org)— "a grassroots nonprofit organization devoted to supporting philosophical inquirers of all ages…"

Be an active and engaged listener.
Respect the ideas of each participant.
Encourage participants to offer specific examples that back up what they believe to be universally accepted views.
Inquire of others' perspectives.
Make sure all have a chance to speak.

Be receptive to unexpected or unfamiliar responses.

Utne Reader Salons – (www.utne.com/salon)—a wide ranging resource for forming groups interested in arts, politics, environment, media and more.

Help keep the discussion on track.
Address remarks to the group, not the leader.
Listen carefully to others.
Speak freely without monopolizing.
Maintain an open mind.
Let go of preconceived ideas.
Legitimate silence.
Listen to your body as a cue to speak.

Etc!

I love the diversity of these perspectives! And these are just a smattering of the groups out there. But this gives you an idea of the burgeoning interest in dialogue. Hurray! If you're interested, you <u>can</u> find a group to join.

The Self-Organizing Universe

The quote, at the beginning of the chapter, is one of my favorites. It's been quoted in many different ways from many others interested in group process. But always it is simple and poignant. In ten simple words, it condenses the sentiments of dialogue. "Be there" asks you to show up and remain in the present moment with the people and the words that are being spoken. "Speak the truth," asks you to contribute what you know or believe, free of fear or ulterior motive. "Let go of the outcome," asks that when you leave the circle you recognize and respect the wisdom of the group. No, you don't have to accept it—but you mustn't undermine it. If you have shown up—and if you have spoken your truth and the group reaches a different conclusion from you—it's OK. All have benefited from the truths that were spoken. All have increased their worldliness, relative to the topic. You've strengthened connections with your peers. You're still alive and kicking. And the universe is self-organizing anyhow, so what will be will be—regardless of one's best-laid plans.

And that is all right too. *It really is.*

Stop reading at the end of this paragraph. Get a drink of water. Stretch. Take a few deep breaths. Walk around your yard or living space. Review the varying perspectives of the dialogue groups above. Which appeal to you? Are you ready to broaden your horizons by joining a dialogue group? Follow the links from one of the websites above or do some research in your local paper or library for groups forming. Nothing appeal to you? Start your own! Read <u>The Joy of Conversation—The Complete Guide to Salons</u> by Jaida n'ha Sandra or <u>Turning to One Another</u> by Margaret Wheatley for other ideas. Then send out a broadcast email and put an ad in your paper under "meetings & workshops." See what develops.

Chapter 16

The Ecology of Vision

"Suppose that we were able to share meanings freely without a
compulsive urge to impose our own view or to conform to those of others
and without distortion and self-deception. Would this not constitute a
real revolution in culture and therefore eventually in society?"
David Bohm, <u>Changing Consciousness</u>, 1992[21]

It's clear that the guidelines for dialogue, from the previous chapter, were created from vastly different realms. Nonetheless, there are strong reoccurring themes that form their base:

Agreeing on a topic and remaining with it,

Being present physically, mentally and emotionally / deep listening,

Revealing your truth,

---

[21]   Bohm, David. and Edwards, Mark. <u>Changing Consciousness</u>. Scranton, PA: HarperOne, 1991.

Avoiding judgment of others' truth / maintaining an open mind,

Practicing compassion / maintaining an open heart,

Honoring and learning from diverse perspectives,

Slowing down the conversation / welcoming silence,

Actively seeking commonality in others' perspectives, and

Maintaining faith in a collective wisdom.

Seven Generations Hence

These tenets comfort me. They give me faith in the future of humanity and remind me of many Native American traditions of interaction. In the ritual passing of the talking stick, each member's words are heard and honored. Diverse perspectives are sought and considered. Before decisions are finalized, they inquire of the collective body, "what effects will our actions and decisions have on the next seven generations?"

Dialogue, the most satisfying of interactions, makes possible this degree of discernment. Yet we mustn't beat ourselves up for struggling with the concept or mastery of the skill. For the typical gathering attended by those of us educated in the Western world is characterized—to greater or lesser degrees—by debate. It's a cultural norm. Why? We were educated in debate—not dialogue. In fact, we got scholastic credit for debate and were encouraged to join the debate team for extra credit. That means we got to *ignore, negate and malign* the voices of our friends and colleagues for the reward of good grades and approval by our elders! Yikes. No wonder dialogue skills are so foreign. No wonder many of our interactions—up until now—were so hollow. No wonder we're at war.

I'm encouraged that dialogue groups are sprouting up everywhere—at an accelerating pace. And I'm thrilled that we have elected a president who not only talks the talk, he walks it—encouraging dialogue through his words, actions and website. Leading up to the election, I volunteered to canvass the campus of a state university. Several students with a video camera—probably from a political or social science class—approached me and asked for an interview. I thought "why not?"

Among other things they asked me why I was supporting my candidate. "I want a president whose respect for all humanity gains respect for this country; someone who doesn't judge based on differences in faith or custom or political views; someone who willingly and courageously engages other world leaders, despite our differences; someone who listens and learns and respects diverse voices; someone who connects; someone who recognizes that violence is always a last resort; a leader who makes me proud to be an American."

I realized later that I was echoing the tenets of dialogue.

Stop reading at the end of this paragraph. Get a drink of water. Stretch. Take a few deep breaths. Walk around your yard or living space. Get pad and paper or journal. Have a dialogue with yourself. E.g., let the ideas, thoughts and feelings flow without edit. Ask yourself "what outcomes do I desire through richer conversation?" If you get stalled at 10, walk around 'til the brain cells begin to brew again. Then add 5 more, then 5 more.

This is your roadmap.

Conclusion

The Ecology of the Journey

"One does not discover new lands without consenting to lose sight
of the shore for a very long time."
(Andre Gide)

Dear One,

If you are reading this letter, it means you've faithfully completed your itinerary toward rich, relevant and generative conversation. In so doing, you've navigated your inner ecology of thoughts and words—and explored their influence on those in your outer ecology: family, friends, colleagues, and community, et al. In all likelihood, the journey has been arduous at times— for you've identified and reassessed long held beliefs, feelings, attitudes and judgments. This has required real courage and a willingness to expose vulnerabilities. If you have, subsequently, experienced turbulence along the way—congratulations! It means you dug deep into your ecology. I do hope you've enjoyed the adventure.

Perhaps you're feeling vulnerable. Good! That means you've discovered aspects of yourself long buried. Your identity may be shifting. Stay with it.

Perhaps you're feeling excited. Good! It means you're preparing for a plunge into even deeper waters. Be courageous.

Perhaps you're feeling fear. Good! Embrace it. It's part of the human experience. You have lots of company. Share it and feel the warmth of commonality.

Perhaps you're feeling peaceful. Good! It means your heart is open and you're ready to welcome newness into your life.

Probably you're experiencing a bit of everything. I encourage you to pick up your journal and—you guessed it—record your thoughts and feelings. Remember—what you resist persists, so open your arms to all the new possibilities ahead. The act of writing neutralizes the negatives and solidifies the positives. It generates creative thinking.

Please know that you have not completed the journey. You, like I, still have a long way to go. We'll still experience occasional instability in the heavens. This is life, after all, and we are only human. Forgive yourself if you sometimes lose your way.

You've acquired skills and knowledge that allow you to embrace, experience and profoundly influence the health and well-being of your "ecosystem." As such, you are primed for authentic, soulful and generative conversations with yourself and others. Keep moving forward in your quest and maintain your faith. Continue to clear your path of cobwebs. Keep your eyes, ears and heart open. Little by little, through your generosity of spirit and open heart, you really *can* change the world.

With Abundant Love and Blessings,
Judi

Afterword

A Word With New Facilitators About Facilitation

With my tennis team, I attended a weeklong clinic back in the mid-80's. On Hilton Head Island, we practiced our shots all day, partied every evening, dropped into bed at night, then started all over again the next day. We had a blast, but the intent of the week was ultimately somewhat lost—a result of receiving so much instruction on so many shots in the course of a short five days: ground stroke, lob, volley, half-volley, forehand, backhand, slice serve, flat serve, serve and volley, topspin, under spin. Egad! It was just too much information in too short a period. My game went to hell! It took a year to get it back. There is one skill, however, that I acquired and maintained. You might call the following one of my one-minute-stories.

Once a day, the owner of the facility, Dennis Van Der Meer, would address all the teams—with words of wisdom, concerning the game of tennis. One afternoon he said, "If you want to win the match, then never take your eyes off the court." These words have consistently helped me to beat better players. When I'm in a tough match, I block out everything beyond the side and base lines. This includes the sky, the spectators, the players on the next court—everything.

This message fittingly transfers to the art of group facilitation. The best facilitators block out everything but what's occurring and what's being spoken within the circle. They roll with the punches, they check in frequently with the group, they have a plan—so they can divert from it, if necessary. They keep their eyes and ears in the here and now.

In the second half of The Ecology of Conversation, you've received a crash course in facilitation. Like my week at the tennis clinic, you've brushed the surface of the skill sets necessary to be a competent facilitator. More than anything, competency requires individualized training, practice and mentoring. A previous employer, Executive Adventure, Inc, provided my training in facilitation. Thomas Sappington, PhD. mentored me. I have a Masters Degree in Team and Leadership Development. The material in this book is the result of the experiences of 23 years of involvement in group-process.

I share this because many believe facilitation is easy. It isn't. I liken it to the art of meditation—a skill that takes dedicated and regular practice. So, if you want to facilitate and are, as yet, unskilled in facilitation, I encourage you to tread lightly. Please— no personal agendas! If you're uncertain about your skills, enroll in a course and/or find a mentor. Then, with time, you can help groups to change the world.

Voila!

Acknowledgements

I have many to thank.

My friend, Diann Schindler, Ph.D.—for your generous insight, meticulous editing, encouragement and space for writing. You fanned the flame and gave me safe haven to write. My friends—Patty and Jack Cox. I needed more time and you lent me your cabin, with the purity of love I can always count on. My friend and colleague, Thomas Griggs, Ph.D.—for introducing me to the Chaos Theory. It continues to give me faith. My sister Barbara Mills, Ph.D.—you've always been there for me. You're a great model for courage, compassion, reflection and inquiry. My Mom, Elisabeth H. Utter—for my original inspiration. If we were alike, I'd probably be doing something else with my life. My friend and colleague, the late Ray Daley—your authentic presence made you an unforgettable role model for everything you stood for. I miss you.

My friends and clients in Executive Dinner Forum—in particular: Chris Kleyla, Rick Anicetti, Butch Aggen, Lee Balance, Debbie Lee Averitt, Lennart Blomdahl and Dave Sutherland—for believing in EDF and providing me with such rich experiences.

My creative inspiration, Julia Cameron[22]—through your words, I've pushed myself further than I ever thought possible. My spiritual guide, Paul Ferrini[23]—your words ground me every single day of the year.

My husband and life partner, Kevin Beck—for role modeling dedication to the creative life, reading and rereading my manuscript, and being here for the duration. You're my hero.

---

[22]   Cameron, Julia. <u>The Artist's Way</u>. NY: Jeremy P. Tarcher / Penquin, 2002.

[23]   Ferrini, Paul. <u>Love Without Conditions</u>. Greenfield, MA: Heartways Press, 1994.

Recommended Reading

In addition to the books footnoted ...

David Abram, Spell of the Sensuous (Knopf Doubleday, NY, 1997).

Christina Baldwin, Life's Companion (Bantam, NY, 1990).

Julia Cameron, The Vein of Gold (Putnam, NY, 1996).

Stephen Covey, The Seven Habits of Highly Effective People (Fireside / Simon & Schuster, NY, 1989).

Natalie Goldberg, Writing Down the Bones (Shambhala, Boston, 1986).

Muriel James and Dorothy Jongeward, Born to Win (Addison Wesley, MA, 1973).

Derrick Jensen, Listening to the Land (Sierra Club Books, San Francisco, 1995).

Bill Moyers, Healing and the Mind (Doubleday, NY, 1993).

Barack Obama, The Audacity of Hope (Random House, NY, 2006).

Gary R. Renard, The Disappearance of the Universe (Fearless Books, Berkley, CA 2003).

Theodore Roszak, The Voice of the Earth (Touchstone, Simon & Schuster, NY, 1992).

Don Riso and Russ Hudson, The Wisdom of the Enneagram (Bantam, NY, 1999).

Margaret Wheatley, Leadership and the New Science (Berrett-Koehler, San Francisco, 1992).

Margaret Wheatley, A Simpler Way (Berrett-Koehler, San Francisco, 1996).

About the Author

Judi Beck has navigated the field of human development for 23 years. She has a Master's degree in Team and Leadership Development with a concentration in Ecopsychology. Her clients include individuals and teams from Fortune and International 500 companies. She's a freelance writer and has been published in *Pastel Artist International (currently Pastel Journal)*, *The Inner Edge*, *Philanthropy International*, The Inner Edge Book of Practices, and countless corporate and regional publications. The Ecology of Conversation is her first book. She and her husband, artist Kevin Beck, live in the Blue Ridge Mountains of North Carolina.

Photographs by Ben Henderson

Judi Beck